I WAS BORN IN LOUISIANA

WALTER D'ALESSANDRO

Ordering Information:

Prime Seven Media
518 Landmann St.
Tomah City, WI 54660

Printed in the United States of America

Look at men
not from the side they show
but from the side they conceal.

Lucius Anneus Seneca

TABLE OF CONTENTS

CHAPTER 1

"Good morning. My name is John Reginald Powell."

A black man, about six feet tall with short curly hair and a sculpted physique, showed up at the police department one ordinary Saturday morning.

Dawn had just broken. The sun had barely begun to illuminate New York's buildings and heat up what would become a pleasant, warm late Spring weekend.

The black man had entered the main building just as the first rays of the day, slipping through two buildings, hit the front door of the department, illuminating it with a bright, blinding light.

Through that ethereal glow, the officer on guard was only able to catch a glimpse of a shadow, a tall and mighty silhouette, materializing against the light. It was enveloped by light so that for a moment he had the sensation of being witness to a divine apparition.

There, in the hall, everything was still relatively quiet, almost silent. The space was shrouded under the dull and lazy routine of the end of the work week.

Until that moment, it had been a relatively calm night at District Number 12. Strangely, only a few calls; some drunkards disturbing the peace, a couple of minor bar fights, family quarrels and neighbourhood noise complaints. In one of the cells were a couple of boys who had been found attempting to sell a few grams. In short, nothing unusual.

Until John Reginald Powell entered.

He, on the other hand, had had a very unserene night indeed. In the last twenty-four hours something terribly unexpected had happened, something that had suddenly stifled all his dreams and thrown him, for whatever reason, into a spiral of deep despair.

Suddenly, in every inch of his existence and soul, anguish and madness had taken over in the place of reason.

And so the tall, imposing Mr. Powell crossed the hall very slowly, dragging his feet.

He lurched forward slowly, with wide lethargic steps, swaying jerkily like a canoe responding only to the current and the pull of the oars.

He made his way inside the precinct, and stopped in front of a counter where an neatly uniformed officer was excellently performing his task of first reception and sorting.

Only then was the officer finally able to put a face to the figure, and clearly distinguish its features. His eyes were wide and glazed over but, at least in appearance, perfectly alert. His beard was bristly and unkempt. On his face, clear as day, was the frenzy of fury and hatred.

He stared aimlessly with a slightly downcast gaze and large dilated pupils streaked with red that gave the impression of wanting to jump out of their sockets at any moment, making his appearance even more chilling.

Frightened, the officer looked into that face. Corrugated eyebrows, rigid, dilated nostrils, teeth clenched almost to the point of crumbling, and tight lips. He noticed that the veins in the man's neck were swollen and pulsating, and his jaw was trembling with tension. On that morbid, middle-aged face was an infinite, palpable evil.

His face was livid, his forehead lightly dotted with conspicuous blood splatters mixed with droplets of sweat that glistened, illuminated by the dismal neon lights of that gray, airless department entrance.

He was breathing heavily. He breathed in by pulling his shoulders up and held his breath for a moment before emptying his lungs with a gasp. John Reginald Powell was wearing a white T-shirt with some strange, illegible design. Illegible because the shirt was covered in smears of fresh blood.

John Reginald Powell was only eleven years old when his father decided to move to New York City. A long time had passed, but by a strange and perverse play of the mind, at that very moment Reginald felt the vivid ripples of memory of the happiest years of his life rise again. His childhood in the Louisiana countryside, a stone's throw from Baton Rouge. A place that Guy de Maupassant would have called *a suburb of suburbs*.

The gate to the *garden of his memories* swung wide open and he entered, with his imagination, into that peaceful world. He was suddenly reminded of the sound of chirping cicadas in the morning, the warm, radiant sunshine, as he raced along the wheat fields on the road that led to the only bus stop in the town. A school bus for black children only.

That's how it worked. In Louisiana, in the late '70s, there were still school buses for whites and school buses for blacks.

Not everywhere. The world was changing even in rural Louisiana, but not quickly. In those places, in the outskirts and the suburbs, those furthest away, the world moved slower, TVs were few and books and newspapers were a rarity. In those very places, in the deep heart of the most genuine America, minds had been sufficiently exploited and rendered inept and thus indifferent to the passage of time.

Louisiana state laws had slowly changed over the years to promote equality and integration, yet ignorance, pride and arrogance still held sway, and it was people of color who paid that price.

The laws of men and the laws of the state were still quite distinct, and most often conflicting.

Little Reginald, however, was not bothered by it. Or rather, he seemed to barely notice it. His friends in the countryside near Baton Rouge were all black. Children with bright, white smiles shining out of their joyous young faces. That was his universe, and no matter how small it was, it was enough for him; no matter how often it came across as unfair, it was just as joyful for him. He considered it all in all, a pleasant, cheerful and hospitable world.

Little Reginald was sheltered in his carefree bubble, and was unaware that outside his happy slice of Louisiana might lurk a different world.

He had not been touched by it. Not yet.

In that little world he and his friends loved to chase each other through cornfields, climb trees, play hide-and-seek in the tall, swaying grass, in the woods, or behind abandoned cottages that had sometimes collapsed into piles of wood and junk left to rot in the hot sun.

Children who loved to run, in whose veins flowed a sense of freedom, who loved to feel the wind touch their cheeks and soothe the burning of the blazing Louisiana sun.

And then there was Marion, the most beautiful child, the one with the sweetest smile, who often visited his dreams.

At night, she always appeared. He would see her so clearly, dressed in sweetness and a red dress that fluttered lightly in the wind. He dreamed of rushing up to her to hold her, embrace her and roll playfully in the grass.

He would sometimes dream of kissing her as he had seen his parents do so many times, with a short, soft, gentle touch of her lips to his.

He barely knew what those delicate touches meant, but he had noticed the tenderness it instilled in his mother and father every time they exchanged a kiss.

He would wake up and feel her lying next to him or, sometimes, he would see her facing the bed, in those brief moments when the gentle morning light would filter through his eyelids.

She would then reach her hands out to him, her face would light up in a beautiful, ethereal smile, and just as the tips of their fingers seemed about to touch, just as he felt he could reach out and hold her tight, that vision would disappear again, giving way to the ruthless sunlight of a new day.

He would feel his heart pound, invaded by that strange and powerful energy that wrenched Marion from his imagination and uprooted his soul to carry it away on the angelic wings of his dream world.

To little Reginald this did not bring sadness. It all made sense, for he had his *Tyche*, his very own personal goddess of fortune to wish him good morning.

Marion was there at the end of his dream each time. She was there to greet the beginning of a new day.

He would spend his mornings waiting to see her, and his young heart would beat fast when he met her, with their other friends after school under the large elm tree at the crossroads of the great tractor road.

That's what they called it, *the great tractor road.*

They called it that because, when the torrid season began, a huge number of large tractors and harvesters would pass through, heading to the fields to do work that served to enrich the landowners, the white men in fancy clothes and glistening cars.

Reginald had no inkling of this, for he lived in a corner of the world that managed to keep inequality out, a world where racism could not enter. This was also thanks to Mom and Dad, Natalie and Joseph, who had tried hard to ensure that nothing and no one could burst Reginald's bubble.

To him, those tractors were just steel monsters to run away from, to play hide-and-seek with, to race against.

With black fumes emanating from their powerful engines, the tractors started off with an advantage, but those huge wheels could not always outrun pairs of thin little legs full of energy, joie de vivre, and a desire for freedom.

Reginald would win; sometimes he would win first place.

When he did, he would raise his hands to the sky and jump up to get the driver's attention, to jeer at him, to say, "I won today, you know? And next time I will win again."

Immediately afterwards he would run to Marion. He had to bring her the news, and inform her of his victory. It was absolutely necessary. Even when she witnessed the scene, he would still run to her to collect his prize. The prize was her smile.

The reaction of the little girl was always the same. A bright and angelic smile. It had some mischief in it, despite her tender age.

John Reginald Powell could not meet her gaze in those moments. He had learned that eyes are a window to the soul.

So he would lower his gaze, because his shyness did not allow him to say what she already knew very well.

His heart would beat timidly, nourished by a pure love, without impulses or passions. His love was tender, gentle and selfless.

CHAPTER 2

For we know that the law is spiritual: but I am carnal, sold under sin.
For that which I do I allow not:
for what I would, that do I not;
but what I hate, that do I

Saint Paul the Apostle, Romans 7:14-15

On his face, the conspicuous splashes of blood were now mixing with sweat, taking on the consistency of slime trickling slowly down his cheeks.

Cuts were visible on his large, muscular arms, from which blood was still dripping. It slid down past his elbows. Small fragments of glass were visible under the skin; the cause of the slow bleeding. The guard stationed at the entrance could see no further than the arms.

His jeans, held up by an old, worn leather belt were covered by the high counter.

"Do you know what I did, officer? Do you have any idea of what happened tonight?" He spoke in a sarcastic and contemptuous manner. The officer was a tall, lanky young man, fresh out of the Academy. His inexperience showed in the way he stood for a few moments petrified, terrified. He did not respond to the man's question.

"Ok, now get off your ass and call someone."

Powell bent down slowly and gently let the bloodstained axe he was clutching in his right hand slide to the floor. Rising again, he stretched out both arms over the counter and brought his wrists together.

Powell had fought against his demons, and then had fought physically against someone who had fallen under his blows. He wanted to be arrested; he had to curb his rage, his fury, his madness. In a single flash of clarity he felt the overpowering desire to be stopped. He knew there was no other way. The feat he had just carried out was a tragedy.

Tonight there will be no more murders, no more horrors, he seemed to want to say. *Do not wait for more crimes to be committed. The forces of evil tonight dominated me, and only me. I am the Monster.*

He had come into the department to prove to everyone that the wickedness of New York City had flowed that night into the soul of its best, most appropriate candidate.

A drop of blood slowly slid down his little finger and soiled the paper resting on the counter. The officer had followed its slow, languid movement with bated breath.

He remained petrified for a few seconds. Inexperience made his heart beat as he stared at the man.

He had not seen Powell's axe but had heard its thin, metallic clang as it reached the floor. An iron clanging of the kind that seeps into the ears and then into the brain. A subtle and powerful hiss, capable of extinguishing any will, of interdicting any movement. It was followed by a thud, a wooden thump, dark and dull, caused by the wooden handle.

The officer had no idea what John Reginald Powell could have been up to with that contraption. He trembled in front of that emaciated face, that purplish-red river of blood.

He could see the axe in his mind's eye, now that it rested on the floor. Imagination did not have to try very hard. Though he knew he could not be certain, he had absolute conviction as to what had happened.

His thoughts took over, and he was catapulted into the unknown depths of his mind, full of dark and imposing shadows.

He imagined the sinister gleam of the blade, saw the tormented man hurl himself violently at an undefined body. He saw with hazy clarity an unknown and innocent victim give way under the violent blows of that deadly axe. He could almost hear the screams.

"How could this have happened?" Powell spoke to himself. Then, after a brief pause, he turned back to the policeman. "I told you, arrest me!"

The officer awoke from his restless flow of thoughts, and was pulled back into the lobby, as if awoken from a nightmare.

He stared at the man again, motionless, his arms still outstretched, his wrists still joined in front of him.

John Powell held both meanness and exhaustion in his swollen, bloody face, drenched in sweat. In spite of everything he still held the macabre and extraordinary magnificence which belongs to all that is *untamable*.

Then he took a slow, deep breath and tried to re-engage his mental faculties. He looked more closely at the face of that self-reporting killer whose crime was yet to be known; he noticed, suddenly, that it was not the face of a monster at all.

John Reginald Powell's attitude was losing intensity, nor did it seem sociopathic.

The human mind cannot stop making analogies, cataloging, classifying; establishing an order to all things. That face did not belong to any of the categories of criminals studied at the police academy. He did not look like a serial killer, a psychopath, a maniac or a predator. John Reginald Powell seemed now mild mannered, a good neighbor, who for some reason that night had abandoned the path of common sense and taken a turn into the absurd, the irreparable.

Something had overwhelmed him to the point of rupturing the depths of his soul, to the point of violating so horribly the boundaries that separate life from death.

He had fought his demon and won. Or perhaps he had lost. More plausibly, they had both lost.

Then what? What had caused that gentle giant to take an axe and strike, to kill with abandon?

Suddenly, the officer's moment of turmoil vanished, and a certain calm came over him. Inexplicably, he no longer felt fear clutching at his stomach.

Without realizing it, for just a moment, he felt pity for that murderer; that violent, bloodstained, foul-smelling, exhausted human being; the man with a mean face and aggressive attitude, who had entered the police department with a bloody axe. That black man, muscular, wounded, seemed to him now incomprehensibly harmless.

For a moment he felt confused; he did not understand whether in front of him was a meek man hiding a dark side or a dark man preserving a meek side.

He was sure of one thing at the very least: *every man holds within himself the mysteries of evil and the miracle of salvation.*

He felt persuaded. He must have read it somewhere. He felt protected from fear. He could not, however, completely interrupt his thoughts.

Powell unexpectedly clenched his teeth and flared his nostrils. His eyes widened, he raised his arms high above his head, still holding his wrists together, and violently beat down with his fists against the counter.

The drops of blood under his palms splattered in every direction, onto the papers, onto the counter. A few small flecks reached the officer, he felt the moisture against his cheeks.

"ARREST ME, FOR GOD'S SAKE!" cried Powell.

In that instant, there was a thunderous murmur inside the 12th District police department; everyone turned around and caught sight of the tall, grimy black man with a bloodstained axe resting at his feet.

Some officers instinctively brought their hands to their hips and opened the gun holster in a fluid, spontaneous gesture; no one, however, actually drew their weapon.

The officer at the counter reacted rapidly and signaled his colleagues to halt. Everything was under control.

"What happened, sir, who did you kill?" he asked, flaunting a certain nonchalance in the face of that questioning.

"Wrong question, Newbie. The question should be *why.*" retorted Powell, with a hint of nervousness.

"All right. I'd better call someone for you," replied the officer.

He kept his composure. Fortunately, Powell's aggressive gesture had failed to shake his conviction. On the contrary, he was now even more certain.

'Something happened' he thought. Something had turned this man into a monster.

The human soul is full of hidden folds. The reason for Powell's actions was hidden in one of these folds, giving free rein to madness.

Madness is often latent and occurs as a result of a specific event. The Academy had taught him. It was a trigger.

He grasped the telephone and dialed the number without looking, while staring straight into the eyes of the man before him with chilling composure.

CHAPTER 3

*What is the highest and most valuable good
attainable through our own actions?
Happiness.*

Aristotle

The tree house.

God, the tree house! How to forget it. The perfect refuge, the vault of secrets, the hidden world of the children, made up of haphazardly nailed boards that stood together, testing the laws of physics.

Adults admonished the children not to go up there. The tree house was old, built by who knows who and now perilously unsafe.

But it was their palace, their little castle. They felt like kings and queens, knights and ladies; sometimes they were brave heroes rescuing little mermaids in trouble; sometimes they were cooks, cooking for their husbands and playing house.

In the tree house, many scents wafted up and mingled. Corn, flowers, thick foliage, and the wind, which brought with it the Southern warmth and dust. But above all, John Reginald Powell and his friends breathed in the scent of happiness. Merging, all those scents intoxicated their young souls with endless joy and delight.

They would climb that rickety staircase and step through the door between creaks and groans and dangerously rotting wood, crossing the boundary of the real world to dive into a world of fantasy, games and fairytales.

Many tales were told in that childlike, innocent world.

"You know, yesterday I saw a UFO. Before I went to bed I looked out the window and saw a big luminous disk standing still in the sky, right in front of me. I wanted to wave at it but it flew away and disappeared over the roof at the speed of light."

"So they exist?"

"Sure they do, what do you think? It's not like we're the only ones in the whole universe."

"Well, I woke up tonight and there was a Slender-man in my room."

"What's a Slender-man?"

"A tall, terrible dark man with a deep voice and two very long, powerful arms. He uses them to grab you and eat you up."

"Christ, what did you do?"

"I leapt out of bed, grabbed my sword, and chased him away. What else could I have done?"

A smile appeared on Powell's face right then. For some reason, being locked up in interrogation room 2 had isolated his thoughts enough to bring it back to those wonderful memories. For a while, the drama of that night had faded, disappeared.

The happy and serene memories of his childhood had come to his rescue again. It allowed him a small moment of respite, isolation and detachment from the real world.

That night evil had overtaken Powell's heart and his innocence had disappeared, yet the gate to the *garden of memories* was still wide open, and upon entering he had found his innocence there, under that big tree, on the *great tractor road.*

Suddenly the door swung open with a grating sound.

Detective Mark Alessi stood in the doorway, his hand on the doorknob, scrutinizing the man hunched over under the white lights, splashes of blood on his face, and a mild look of resignation.

He stepped into the room.

CHAPTER 4

The demon is that soul which, when freed from all disturbances and errors, lives in its own nature and its own freedom.

Marcus Aurelius

"They tell me this belongs to you."

FBI detective Mark Alessi entered the interrogation room holding a plastic bag marked "EVIDENCE." He held it aloft, with his arm stretched forward, to assure that the confessed offender could distinguish it clearly. Inside the envelope was the bloody axe, the one that John Reginald Powell had laid on the ground after entering the department.

Detective Alessi noticed that Powell barely deigned to take a glance. He knew all too well what the bag contained. The detective closed the door behind him. Then he took a couple of steps forward and went to place the evidence on the table, with a slow gesture, so it lay before John Reginald Powell, who held an expression still partially transfigured by wrath. In the span of a few seconds, the stench of the stale blood in which Powell was covered rose up his nostrils and pierced Mark Alessi's stomach like an awl. The smell was nauseating, and had filled the entire room. That stench, despite the recent happenings of the night before, already smelled of decomposition.

Detective Mark Alessi felt about to retch and sank his nose and mouth into the crook of his elbow. He remained rigid in that position without breathing. With his tongue on his palate he could clearly distinguish the acrid, metallic, deathly taste of blood. Disgust pervaded him, as if the smell was polluting his body. He was forced to step out of the room for a moment to take a breath, trying to tug his mind away from that feeling and shake himself off.

It was not that he had never smelt blood before, but there, in that nine square metre room, where air ventilation was poor to say the least, he had never expected to affect him so. He could not have predicted it.

That very situation, on that very morning, had been unthinkable. As he slammed the door shut he gagged, then drew a long, slow breath. He held it in for a couple of seconds and expelled the air in one liberating exhale. He barely managed not to retch and empty his breakfast into the hallway, but with a few more gulps of clean air he willed himself back into lucidity. His colleague and friend, Detective Silvio Brugger, just then walked over holding two cups of Americano, black and scalding. Mark immediately grabbed one and gulped half of it down.

"Do we already know who this guy is?" Brugger noticed his colleague's pale face and his extraordinary effort to not throw up. He did not flinch. On the contrary, he hinted at a wry, mocking smile. Then he sipped his coffee.

Mark, meanwhile, had sunk his face into the coffee cup. He breathed in the intense scent; a panacea to chase away the putrid smell. He took another slow sip, to make sure that all the stench had disappeared.

"Apparently upon entering he said his name but the officer on guard was... well... scared stiff, I would say. He doesn't remember."

Silvio re-entered the interrogation room first. Mark waited for a few more moments; he took another mouthful of air.

John Reginald Powell was sitting in his chair wearing a sad, mournful, rough expression. His gaze was directed to the ground, and from this perspective he did not manifest a particularly murderous attitude. He appeared rather as a dejected king, who laid down his arms and decided to surrender himself to the enemy, without real resignation. On the contrary, he seemed to still hold both pride and hatred in his heart, wounded to the core, to the point of crushing his soul.

As he entered the room, Silvio observed Powell at length. He felt a strange sensation; he sensed in John Reginald a kind of dual nature. Nothing to do with a split personality disorder brought up by therapists in some similar situations, but perhaps something more superficial, a trivial character profile, containing two major aspects. Powell had a visibly proud demeanor, and seemed undeniably proud of his *feat*. He felt, with little doubt, that he was a hero. The hero needs extraordinarily desperate circumstances to manifest his valor, he appears out of danger, when all others run away. One does not recognize the hero in calm and stillness, but can rather distinguish him in the storm.

"How many deranged and desperate ideas come to the mind of a deranged and desperate man?" thought Silvio Brugger. He had read that phrase somewhere and now, in the presence of that killer with a hidden side, it came back to him. He had the feeling that it was particularly appropriate.

Though, perhaps it was not despair, he thought to himself. Perhaps, more realistically, Powell had been a man full of drive, such that over time, day after day, it had been replaced with a sense of distrust, morphing into a skepticism toward the entire human race. A person who may have been full of vitality, but whose vitality had been turning slowly into shadow, dulled by time and a despairing lack of happy occurrences in his life.

Yet this man had, all at once, exploded with a volcanic rage and energy of which the most terrifying of human beings can be capable. This was, without the shadow of a doubt, the confusing and ambiguous image that not only Silvio Brugger, but also his colleague Mark Alessi drew upon observing John Reginald as he sat crumpled on the chair, his legs stretched out under the table, and his wrists manacled and chained to the iron structure on the interrogation table.

"So... " Silvio Brugger began, "you came here of your own free will, covered in blood, with your axe. You have self-reported some heinous and yet undiscovered murder. I have a feeling you should be talking."

He paused briefly. Then he resumed, "... Do you want to start telling us what happened?" asked Silvio Brugger as he slid into the black chair reserved for law enforcement officers. He sat there calmly, fixing his tie in a blatant but habitual gesture.

Moments of silence followed; seconds, then minutes.

Then Powell, head still bowed, suddenly lifted his eyes. His pupils lifted into the highest part of the socket and he cast out his mean gaze, lips slightly raised to the side. A strange and invincible force did not allow him to relax his jaw or open his mouth. His teeth could be heard grinding, sounding as if they were about to shatter.

He began again sweating profusely and shaking. The short chains constricting his wrists began to rattle gently. For a moment he almost seemed in the throes of a seizure.

His head and torso shook, breathing heavily; the airflow of his breath, in those moments, hissed slightly as it passed between clenched teeth.

For a second he gave the impression of being pushed by an overwhelming urge to speak, to spit it all out, confess his evil deeds and also his incomprehensible reasons. But soon afterward he was suffocated by torment, and it pushed everything back to him. His words stuck in his throat, choking him, and his voice was muffled by a sob, the terrible kind that arises when one is victim to a terrible, inhibiting emotion.

Then, with a conspicuous jerk of the shoulders, he drew in a deep breath and raised his head slowly. With a wet, yet proud gaze he stared at the off-white ceiling, made dull and gray by thirty years of neglect, soiled by the thousands of atrocious words spoken in that room. Tears slid down sideways across his cheeks, toward his ears, drawing two silvery, shimmering trails. More followed, and more still.

"Where do you want me to start?" he managed to say, sobbing hoarsely. A single suffering sentence that seemed to slip through his unkempt beard and tight lips.

It was more a gasp than an actual sentence. Powell was slowly trying to regain a shred of mental clarity and composure. That black man chained to the table did not show any repentance, only calm. In truth, he wanted to raze the world to the ground.

CHAPTER 5

Wakefulness is a dream in which one dreams about not dreaming.

Jorge Luis Borges

Imagination took over him. The gate opening onto the *garden of memories* appeared before him whenever the turmoil became unbearable. What a lifeline! What a perfect refuge for his addled mind. Marion's sweet face appeared. In the memory she held his hand and his young heart beat louder than a drum.

She had eyes of the deepest black. He never thought that black could become the color of love. Her eyes were a magnet, powered with an irresistible attraction.   "Can I give you a hug?" he had asked her shyly.

"I would like to wrap you in some of my happiness," he had then whispered under his breath.

"You are already doing that, Reginald," she replied. "If you hug me tight, I will feel the love."

"I am scared, Marion. Like I am too small for love."

"You are eleven Reginald, and I am ten. Do you think love stops at age?"

"I know it's silly. I know that. But I'm afraid that I'm not ready to hold it, like I can't protect it. I don't know how to do it. I'm afraid that love will run away from me."

"You cannot stop yourself from being happy today for fear of being sad tomorrow. Happiness is made up of moments, of emotions. And honestly to me it seems unfair not to enjoy the happy moments for fear of paying a price. Everything has a price, Reginald, and if I have to pay my price then I will. But I want my crumbs of happiness."

"Why crumbs, Marion?"

"Because if it wasn't about crumbs it wouldn't be happiness. I'll tell you one thing, though. Some people say that to appreciate light you have to know darkness but I don't think that's true. I love the light, I let it fill me with joy, sweetness, beautiful things and brilliant scents and a thousand other things."

"But what if darkness comes, Marion? What will you do then?"

"Darkness will not come, Reginald, it will not come if you are with me."

It had never happened. That tender exchange that John Reginald Powell was imagining had never happened.

Imagination is a creature that dwells within us and always looks further than the eyes. Much further. The mind travels far, no matter whether it is *far back* or *far ahead*. If it reaches forward into the future, it is called *imagination* and sometimes takes on the shape of ideals. And when those ideals mix with desire, dreams are born. Those sorts of dreams which you will try with all your might to realize.

If, on the other hand, the wandering mind projects itself into the past, it reveals the soul's urge to savor every single moment as if reliving it, and softening it by the love in one's heart.

Yet now there was a demon clawing at his heart. And his wandering, treacherous mind tried to protect itself by travelling far into his memories, making the past leap out at him again and again, sometimes in its true form, sometimes tainted by the lies of imagination. Those gentle scenes had a strange effect on him, taking him over so strongly that John Reginald Powell could no longer distinguish what was hurting him in reality. He could no longer feel anguish, rage or hatred. He could distinguish only a deep, intimate turmoil that seemed to slowly tear him apart.

Travelling back to Louisiana, to Marion, to cornfields, to the tractors, to his friends in the tree house was like lighting up the darkness he was sinking into with bright, sunny rays. Slowly, Marion faded and became Vanessa. The woman to whom he had really thought of dedicating his entire life. In reality it had been only a small portion of his life, yet she was the woman to whom he had really believed he would give his soul and heart. Sadly, John Reginald Powell had been too young and too enthusiastic at that time to understand that love is often about timing.

In the beginning, she is all you can think about. Everything you do you do it for her and with her. But then, as time goes on, you might forget to cultivate that love, to nurture it. Instead it becomes a stagnant routine, ungrateful monotony, and finally burns slowly and painstakingly toward cold detachment.

Love becomes affection, loving gestures become habitual. Love turns into respect, and care for the smaller things fades away and becomes superfluous.

Some say that love is entering a stage of maturity, of awareness. Perhaps a higher degree that leads into making that love untouchable. Perhaps reaching a level of absolute certainty.

It was not the latter, however, for Reginald.

For him, it was detachment.

CHAPTER 6

Reason wants to pronounce a just verdict, anger wants it to seem just; the verdict he pronounced.

Lucius Anneus Seneca

The detectives had witnessed all kinds of theatrics, shenanigans and lies. Over the many years of their careers, dozens and hundreds of offenders of all kinds had passed through those rooms. Maniacs, mobsters, drug dealers, rapists, robbers, serial killers. Lots of manipulators and mystifiers.

The captain, Simon Bishop, and the detectives Alessi and Brugger, had long since received the vaccine. The antidote against fictitious tales, the one that serves to read through the mask that some people know how to wear expertly. Maybe not the antidote against evil. That one does not exist. Their skin had grown thick with diffidence after so many years in that line of work, and it was almost impossible to shake them. Neither aggression nor fake tears, nor by any means cooperation could soften the detectives.

John Reginald Powell spoke.

"Do you know man's most vicious enemy?" He was sitting, his face still turned toward the ceiling and his eyes softly closed. "It's man."

For a brief moment he stood waiting for an answer but no reaction came from the present company. Those layers of distrust and skepticism had been barely grazed.

Silvio remained neutral, arms folded, as Powell's hands were joined as if in prayer in front of him. Sending a clear message that he would not fall into any trap, the detective touched his green and red striped regimental tie and began to roll it around his index finger distractedly, as if bored. He lifted his chin and gave a nod, urging Powell to continue.

Mark, indulging his habits, was pacing around the table and at times leaning his right hip against the wall behind the suspect. He would stand right in the corner, so as not to be reflected by the mirror. That way he could gesture to his partner without being noticed.

It was the age old and yet still incredibly effective game of the good cop and the bad cop.

Yet Detective Mark Alessi could not seem to stand still. His hands were stuffed in his jean pockets, stowed with trinkets, an AAA battery, a keychain and other small objects. He seemed unable to relax, and always had something to fidget endlessly with.

"I would say let's start with *who you are* and *what you did with that axe before you came here.* Take it one step at a time, okay?"

Mark walked slowly back to the front of the table, behind Silvio, who was sat motionless holding John Reginald Powell's dark, deathly stare.

With a slow pace, Detective Alessi threw a glance at the mirror. He imagined meeting the gaze of Captain Bishop watching from beyond the glass. He had also imagined the man's bewilderment.

In the many years he had worked there, it had never happened that a vicious murderer had turned himself in so spontaneously, showing up personally to the department. Not in those chilling conditions at least... Never with an axe in hand. The mirror betrayed no presence.

"There are some people who are so rich that they know no privations except those they desire themselves," Powell continued faintly. "And sometimes, of their own volition, they don't deprive themselves of anything. They don't know what deprivation is. They want everything!"

"Welcome to New York City, Mr. Powell," Mark Alessi replied sarcastically.

"These people ignore the true nature of their freedom and spend their entire lives in petty transgression. *The worst of all evils is opulence,* said the Philosopher." John Reginald Powell's eyes were now wide open, staring at his reflection in the mirror.

"Sure, sure. Sin is devouring us, and God has assigned to you the thankless task of getting the most hardened sinners out of the way. You're a messenger from God, right?" Mark Alessi was trying to provoke him.

Silvio, meanwhile, had gotten up from his chair and was pacing back and forth with his hands resting on his hips.

"Why do you give all the paranoid schizophrenics to us? Huh?" He tapped a knuckle on the mirror trying to look the other way with his face pressed against the glass and his other hand shielding him from light in an attempt to see who was standing behind it.

"I am neither paranoid nor schizophrenic," Powell protested, gritting his teeth angrily. "Least of all am I a messenger of God. Your God abandoned me years ago."

"Our God? *OUR GOD?* What are you, a religious terrorist?" Alessi wanted some answers now.

"Do you want to tell us something, FOR GOD'S SAKE, WHAT DID YOU DO? WHY ARE WE HERE?" Brugger joined in.

Reginald took a deep breath once more. He held his breath a few moments and answered the detective's angry line of questioning with apparent calm.

"I could tell you a thousand things. People have a habit of lying, you know? They do it all the time, all the time." He let his head drop backwards and stared at the ceiling.

"I could tell you that I am Josh Bright from Savannah, Georgia. Or I could be Ted Speed from Toolafalls, Mississippi. In reality I'm… I'm a man, just a man."

With a round motion he lowered his neck, bowed his head, relaxed his muscles, rolled his shoulders, and began to observe his legs crossed in the shadow of the table, as if they were unknown to him.

For a moment he seemed to want to put himself back into a catatonic state, but soon after he lifted his proud gaze, tensed his chains and with fury he whispered, "But now I ask you, what is a *MAN*?"

He remained sat with a straight back, somber gaze fixed on Detective Alessi. "The human being is but a receiver of stimuli. Millions of perceptions that we can translate into language, but each of us has his own personal understanding. Everyone interprets these in their own way and... they are demonic because, as Marcus Aurelius, the Roman emperor, said: *the demon is that soul that has to be cured and deprived of all disturbance.* The stimuli, the events, and... each of us reacts differently because we are influenced by our own personal experiences, those that have marked our past."

He stopped just as suddenly as he had started. He drew in his breath, clenched his fists, and straightened his back. Powell turned into a raging river of emotion. His eyes were rimmed in red, eyes that revealed the blood, the fury and the terror of that night.

"And when the experiences are demonic...," he resumed in a newly dismissive tone, "...they inevitably lead to the annexation of the soul. Marcus Aurelius was right, the psyche becomes a black sky beyond which and before which love no longer exists. And you feel the need to liberate the soul... Free it from its demon, from that disturbance."

Mark Alessi felt suddenly tired. The madman's outburst were making him feel profoundly uneasy. He had believed that Powell might have been acting on instinct, but this was not about instinctive reactions.

It went deeper than that. Powell spoke of reactions that were well reasoned, if the results of a disturbed soul, and were therefore entirely rational.

John Reginald Powell, in his palpable confusion, was talking about a shadowy zone on the border between reason and folly. A border that perhaps does not even exist. Madness flushes away anguish and torment in order to free reason once again. Madness becomes an outlet valve.

"Reactions are always generated by an interior conflict, Detectives. The conflict that will always exist between the heart and the mind. Sometimes the human being is more instinctive, sometimes he is more rational. Sometimes he loses his reason, overwhelmed by emotions and becomes insane. This happens when hatred and anger creep into the mind to play a master role. It is only natural that failing reason gives way to rage. "

He paused briefly. "As far as I'm concerned –I can tell you that my name is John Reginald Powell. I am not a terrorist and I am not a religious fanatic."

Suddenly he became serious, even though he was confused and his gaze was lost, staring into space. There was no psychopathic gleam in his muted eyes, and his unhinged and furious mood seemed to have subsided. His eyes were, however, still showing signs of pride.

"Do you want answers?"

He tensed, but soon sketched a wicked half-mouthed smile. He lifted his gaze with the intent of showing his mocking laugh to the detectives and his nostrils flared with contempt.

"Then go to Bryant Park," he said between his teeth and lifted his chin to signal the destination.

CHAPTER 7

Don't ask yourself why
People go mad.
Ask yourself why they don't.

Meredith Gray

He could see it. A sunny day, a crystal-clear image, like a painting of the most brilliant yellows. Like the wheat fields, like the sun that shines on everything to the farthest horizon. Yellow that turns blue when the sky, with a sharp cut through the horizon, replaces with crystalline transparency the color of the grain.

The blue glow of the sky races forward and traces the end of the horizon, suspended for a moment, and races back across the sky to form a blue dome, of the most beautiful blue the human eye can hope to experience.

Those were the colors in the countryside of Baton Rouge, his home, the land where he felt he belonged, where he had spent his carefree and wonderful childhood.

He was realizing now that he had lived for years under a sky he had never truly admired. By day or by night.

He could see that as well, memory as clear as a mirror. A warm night, the black sky scattered with stars like speckles of ice, blowing in cool air after a muggy day.

In his memories of the day, admittedly somewhat faded, he was sitting in the shade of a majestic tree, with an opulent frond of green foliage, rich with life. Not only because of the thousands of birds that perched there, but also because its leaves, swaying and trembling in the light breeze, gave the impression that they were speaking.

He sensed a presence to his left but, as is often the case in dreams, the figure was not well defined. Whoever it was, they were there in silence enjoying the same landscape, marveling at those same intense colors. Quietly, with composed grace.

Reginald knew who she was, and though he could not see her properly, his heart was able to recognize, without a shadow of a doubt, her sweet presence. He did not want to turn, he wanted to hold onto the feeling of her smile as she watched him. He turned to his right and saw the great tractors coming from afar. Giants, shooting up trails of black smoke, challenging him to a race.

He accepted the unspoken challenge.

In the memory, which seemed distant and dreamlike, the young John Reginald stood up, shook a few dry leaves and soil off with his hands, and set off, swift, fearless and light as the wind.

He reached the metal giants and flanked one of them, the one that appeared to be the most powerful and majestic of them all.

Young Powell raced; he flew like an eagle with spread wings over the updrafts. He ran so fast it seemed as if his slender legs did not touch the ground.

Soon he won, and he cheered. After a few festive leaps with his hands raised to the sky he ran again. He flew back in the direction of the tree, where the delightful, shifting presence of his memory sat waiting for him.

She had seen it all.

Marion had watched the race and was delighted about the victory, knowing well that he had raced and won for her. Only for her.

He ran and ran, and slowed down just before reaching the tree. He stopped for a moment and turned back to look at the *captain* of that big metal giant of a tractor. The driver smiled complicitly, as if he had sensed from the beginning the goal of the race and had slowed down just enough to allow the child to achieve his heroic victory.

Marion had remained still, if a tad restless, holding her breath as she waited for her hero to return. Reginald rejoined her slowly, catching his breath.

Powell's memory now flourished into more than just a dream. It passed through his mind's eye light and fast, perhaps because it was not entirely truthful. Memory does not work like a printer. It cannot report the facts as they truly are. The psyche allows itself to be voluntarily influenced. In dreams, as in memories, it is transported in less cold waters, warmed and softened by the flavor of our hopes, our desires and our innermost feelings.

Memories as such are intangible, because we can exhume them by adapting each to our moods of the moment without fear of being contradicted.

And so, in dreamlike recollection, without saying a word the two children stared at each other for a long time. They had, perhaps for the first time in their lives, savored every moment of that atmosphere charged with awe and something wonderful they had not felt before.

Then, as if guided by a force, Marion moved forward, put her arms around Reginald's neck, and lightly touched her lips with his. It was an innocent kiss, a childish kiss, the kiss a little girl gives a little boy.

Reginald knew, through his religious education, that within each human being God puts a soul, and from it the body can draw life.

At that moment, precisely the second Marion's lips touched his own, little Reginald felt clearly that their two souls had merged. From two was born one. And it was electrifying and charged with ancestral energy.

The union of two souls felt like a miracle, united by the God of love or some God capable of bringing to fruition wonders beyond imagination.

It did seem like a miracle that this girl for which he had yearned and dreamed of was right in front of him.

"*A miracle,*" he would often think of it throughout his life. That a simple touch of tender lips with tender lips can trigger electric shocks, vibrations, emotions such as those he felt in that moment. How their meeting can so quickly enter the heart and mind, and allow the soul to leave the *I* for a second, and introduce it to the unknown and thrilling world of *Us*.

It had thus happened, thanks to Marion, that John Reginald Powell had discovered love. The pure and innocent kind, the genuine love that unites one half with its other half.

But he opened his eyes and the memory flew away.

He realized that he was unable to distinguish whether he had truly experienced those feelings decades earlier in Baton Rouge or whether they were only now expanding in his daydreaming, in the movie of remembrances that his mind was projecting to him, to provide him with a gentle lifeline, to which he could cling onto in the agonizing storm that almost choked him as he sat in the police precinct, awaiting his judgement.

He would have given anything for that Louisiana blue sky to materialize now on the ceiling of that small detention room. He looked up and saw once again the dull gray of a filthy ceiling, soiled by hatred and resentment.

He felt a sense of total alienation from humankind.

The agony and torment were on the verge of suffocating him. It was absolutely the most unacceptable thing he could have ever experienced. The pain cut off his breath.

Unacceptable were the events that had unleashed his madness, unacceptable the madness that had turned into ferocity, unacceptable the ferocity that had caused the river of hatred and anger to overflow in such dissent.

Unacceptable was the massacre and all the other events that had twisted this man and made him into a *monster.*

With his head clenched in his shackled hands, John Reginald Powell was still brimming with anger, but at the same time he sensed the emptiness and abandonment of his soul as it allowed agony and despair to surge within him.

Anguish; what you feel when you plummet into a void and have nothing to hold on to. What you feel when you look at the world around you and realize that salvation, for you, does not exist.

"I killed. Why?"

Above all, this was the question that was now eating at him from within. That inner *I* that some call consciousness and others call soul, could not keep quiet.

He would never have been able to accept all that had come to be in the last few hours of his life. Killing had seemed to him the right thing to do. His body and limbs had appeared to be the proper tools for action. With the help of an axe.

"How could this have happened?" Powell questioned. His mind brought back only jumbled scenes, memories shrouded in fog.

He wondered why that situation had nothing real about it. It seemed to him but a nightmare he had barely woken up from.

Anguish often succeeds in overpowering emotion and reason, until reason itself returns by penetrating inside the unconscious and guiding it toward the light.

But Powell did not see the light. Not yet.

His memories were throwing his mind into disarray. All he could see were gray, blurred outlines as they overlapped tumultuously, taking on the appearance of a cursed nightmare.

A blur.

These are the same hormones that induce self-defense. Fear, the spirit of self-preservation. The instinct of survival which intervenes on the mind to erase traumatic events from memory. After a road accident, witnesses barely remember. After a while, it was memory itself that came to the rescue of his confused mind.

He managed to push his torment to the side, out of the eye of the storm, where everything is taken and destroyed, crushed by the tremendous flurry of events.

After the long and painful contemplation, his fatigued body found a sense of relief, his muscles relaxed, his veins deflated, his hatred dematerialized.

Powell clenched his fingers and grasped his hair; he tightened his wrists against his temples, making a circular motion, applying gentle pressure. A gentle massage aimed at facilitating the return of sweet, beautiful and serene memories.

CHAPTER 8

"I was born crying while all laughed. I die laughing while they all weep."

Jim Morrison

*P*olice cars arrived at Bryant Park from the south side. They were in single file, with their flashing lights on but without the din of sirens, in respectful silence.

They already knew what they would find and where. Powell's instructions had been far too detailed.

Mark Alessi and Silvio Brugger opened the car doors and got out slowly, looking around conspicuously. It was early morning, and as usual on Sundays, the area was still uncrowded.

Bryant Park is a small green lung in the center of Manhattan. Nothing like Central Park, but a much appreciated garden nonetheless, especially by tourists.

The area is full of bars, restaurants, clubs and stores nestled between modern buildings made of shimmering glass, reaching up to the clouds, teeming with life like ant hills.

This is only on weekdays.

On weekends, on the contrary, only tourists go to Bryant Park to crowd the tables placed along the perimeter, and it's well known that vacationers in the early morning are sleeping soundly in their warm hotel beds.

Silvio lifted his head. He had never been in that area in the early morning. He stood for a few moments admiring the display as the sun rays bounced between the mirrored windows of two huge crystal skyscrapers, one a little more irregularly shaped than the other but equally imposing,

Mark, on the contrary, had always been a keen observer. He loved to notice the smallest details, photographing with his mind everything that could be observed at a crime scene.

A couple of children were playing with an orange ball, watched by a woman with long black hair who kept taking pictures of them with her phone.

Further on, a boy was throwing a frisbee to a small dog with a shiny coat, perhaps a pomeranian, who was prancing and running and bursting with energy.

On a bench to the east, curled up, a person was sleeping with a hat thrown haphazardly over their face.

Bryant Park is also a place where sometimes people stay overnight, despite themselves. Kids who flock to parties, discos, and the Big Apple's thousand clubs.

It sometimes happens that some of them, drunk, will lie down on a bench or on the green grass and stay there until the hangover has passed, which normally happens long after the sun has fully risen.

John Reginald Powell had been of few words but the content had been crystal clear.

"On the south side of the park there are four benches in a row," he had said. "On the second one from the right, with your back to the buildings, you will find a man wearing a dark, elegant coat. It will seem to you as if he is sleeping. But he isn't. Or rather, he's sleeping for eternity."

He had underlined the last sentence with the purest of evil. The psychopath's glint had returned behind Reginald's black eyes.

There he was, exactly where Powell had indicated. A handsome, bleached-blond boy, about twenty-four or twenty-five years of age, very well groomed, elegant, and pale.

Deathly pale.

As they approached, the detectives and the forensics team immediately noticed the slightly unnatural bending of the body, the visibly violet outline of the eyes, and above all, a pool of black, stale blood that spread out under the bench.

The coat had been fastened with a belt. The wound that had caused that bleeding was definitely underneath it, but was not visible.

Mark Alessi went back in his mind, thought back to the axe brought by Powell to the department, and decided that he did not want to be the one to open that belt. He had already reconstructed a hypothetical sequence of events.

The axe, the power of John Reginald Powell's blows, the terrified boy, his young face sculpted by fear, his body torn by the violent blows.

He waited for the forensics team to complete an initial series of shots, positioned himself to the side of the bench, on the right side of the corpse, and motioned Silvio to open the overcoat.

Detective Brugger very calmly slipped on blue latex gloves and approached the helpless silhouette. He squatted to observe.

A drip of stale blood was dangling from the end of the bench seat. It did not touch the ground, had extended about six inches, solidified, and stopped in mid-air, its tear-shaped outline elongated. Black, bleak, atrociously prophetic.

He came a little closer and positioned himself right in front of the corpse. He observed it more closely.

His face was serene, almost as if he had not suffered at all. He had two light streaks of blood on his eyelids that then descended to his cheeks.

The killer had closed his eyes.

"What a kind gesture, Mr. Powell," Silvio thought to himself. The detective allowed himself a few more seconds. It was his nature. He wanted to understand, to listen, to interpret what that lifeless face, that life gone, could tell. What that boy might have been thinking in the last moments of his young life, cut short by the man with the axe who now sat in a department cell, tainted with putrid blood and sweat.

No one made a sound.

No one said a word, perhaps to respect the mystical silence that normally accompanies death. Or perhaps because, in their hearts, everyone wanted the wait to be as long as possible. Everyone imagined, or rather knew, what they would see when they opened that elegant coat.

Silvio scrutinized the body in its entirety. Well groomed, golden hair; a shirt collar, snow-white; arms folded over his legs; a watch, a Corum with the dial built from a twenty-dollar coin in gold; the exquisite shoes with the Prada logo barely visible.

The detective summoned some courage and quickly, with purpose, approached the corpse, shifted his arms, resting them the sides on the body, grabbed the belt and pulled it to himself with a sudden, sharp tug.

The coat burst open like a dam that suddenly yields to the force of water and out came a fleshy, bloody mass, teeming with hacked up organs, torn flesh and clotted blood that formed a horrifyingly foul smelling black sludge.

Silvio Brugger quickly snapped backward, shocked, struck to the heart by that hideous, stomach-churning vision. He fell backward, onto the lawn, holding his hands out to keep from falling onto his back. From a sitting position he quickly moved another meter away, pushing back on his heels, sliding his ass over the lawn.

Yet he could not take his eyes off that macabre mass spilling from the boy's abdomen; he was mesmerized by it.

Mark Alessi, meanwhile, had his hands in his hair. He had also taken a step back and remained paralyzed, wide eyed and horrified. But he could not look at the boy's abdomen. His attention was drawn to the face. That boy seemed now to be wearing a mirthful, playful, almost sneering expression.

Mark Alessi had a strange sensation. He had the impression that that lifeless body had revived for a moment and smiled smugly, as if those organs squirted out had actually been part of an artfully organized prank to sweep the cops off their feet.

But it was not a game.

Mark Alessi stood still for quite a while, pondering the facial expression and why that subtle perception of change had occurred to him.

"His soul," he thought. "Perhaps this young man's spirit was waiting to find peace."

It was a hypothesis.

His guardian angel had been trapped on that bench, waiting to be released and relieved of its post. It had to return to God but could not do so without first revealing to the world the circumstances of its agonizing departure.

When Detective Brugger had pulled the coat wide open, he had not only freed the butchered organs. He had liberated the soul.

It had enabled it to find its way back to the light.

CHAPTER 9

The virtuous man contents himself with dreaming what the evil man accomplishes for real.

Sigmund Freud

ohn Reginald Powell sat in the interrogation room, handcuffed and chained to the table. He had been watching the revolving assembly of detectives and police officers, limiting himself to uttering nothing but the strictly necessary.

They had shown him pictures and questioned him. Some asked him politely, others shouted. They slammed their fists on the table and walked back and forth along an imaginary groove that Powell imagined to have been dug into the floor between the mirror and the table.

Some even spewed insults and profanities at him.

Powell, his soul taken by a glacial freeze, remained indifferent to all of those lines of attack, but found himself face to face with his reflection in the mirror of the small interrogation room.

He stared at himself with a sense of detachment, as if the reflection showed a creature other than himself, and he was absolutely mesmerised by it.

Concentrated and hypnotized, he found that he did not recognize the reflected figure. For it was not him, not anymore.

On the contrary, it seemed like he could see clearly the monster in his reflection, an unclean being that had taken over his body and changed him.

No, perhaps not the body, but the soul. His spirit had become riotous and incapable of surviving in a body that was completely alien to it.

There is no such thing as a body without a soul, and he felt the discomfort. That sweaty, blood-soaked body, that face with bulging eyes, a face creased with hatred and anger, and he hated it.

A strong and painful feeling overcame him. His untamed soul was no longer free, he felt instead that it was imprisoned within a body until the end of his days.

Forced to adapt. He sensed it clearly. His conscience had fought against his instincts and had ended up curling in on itself to try to soothe its own torment. Then it exploded in all its horrific violence.

He would have liked to leave his body there.

"Punish him," he thought, "but let me, let my spirit fly free again, over the fields of Louisiana; let my legs run in the dust again, let my hands go back to caressing the yellow tips of the wheat."

"Once a beautiful man, with a noble and gentle soul, had lived in that body," he thought. "Beautiful in both spirit and body."

It was not vanity, but awareness that he had an attractive, strong physique with graceful features. His sweet manners and bright eyes hinted at an endearing shyness.

How distant that seemed now!

Powell was aware that the best memories are often tied to childhood and the freedom of play, the lightness, the energy and delight. We lose these things, crushed by the weight of responsibility.

"But I didn't run away," he thought. "No. It was life that cheated me, the passage of time that spoiled my beauty, stole my virtues and stripped me of the most precious thing. Love."

Life was again flashing before his eyes, but as he continued to stare at the mirror he began to discern a weary lion, with a mane still worthy of the leader of the pack. And yet, he was accepting surrender, ceasing to roar or fight, and slumping down in the shade of the tree to await the night. That battered man, whose sharp gaze was previously capable of cleaving the air like a torpedo, could only reveal a face decayed by regrets.

So many regrets.

That bright and clear mind had collapsed in the span of a single night. He frowned to concentrate better, and stretched his neck in the direction of the mirror.

He isolated a thought.

"There is no past, no present, and no future," He paused for a moment, breathing it in. "There is only life, in a continuous flow, like a river which we cannot hold back but can only embrace, moment by moment, and let go immediately after."

Panta rei, said Heraclitus. Everything flows.

Surely no human being would ever want to witness his own sunset. He would be too involved as a spectator, too present. It would be a horrible spectacle, made so by the inevitability of the passage of time and the ever-shifting human condition.

John Reginald Powell's twilight was near, even though he was just over the age of fifty. It had been marked by the total abandonment of his mind and the utter subjugation to the power of instinct.

He would have liked to pause his life, for a while, just long enough to catch his breath, rise to the surface and take a breath of air.

He looked at himself again in the mirror. He remembered noticing, when he was still only a child in Louisiana, how different he looked from his father. Joseph Powell had been the same age that John Reginald was now, yet he had always appeared incredibly old to his young son. And he was a child with soft features, not yet furrowed by the passage of time, not yet wrinkled by the pitfalls of life. Different, certainly.

But now that he, too, had reached his fifties, he could not help but recognize in his features and manners the outline and disposition of Joseph, now older and wise as ever.

"Man," he thought. "I look just like him. But my father was good and balanced. He hated violence. So what am I doing here?" He managed, for a few seconds, to create a vacuum of thoughts. He enjoyed the brief inner silence.

"Instincts," he then thought, and at that moment, as if a bell had rung in the synapses of his brain, he shuddered and abruptly changed his attitude again. The killer who had seemed subdued and dormant, rose again powerfully within him.

He returned to focus on the mirror, but this time he did so with the interest and attention with which one observes a work of art.

He scrutinized its details, paid attention to the wrinkles, the ominous signs of time, to the small wounds, still alive and pulsating.

In the short span of a minute, he was flooded by a sense of pride and felt intoxicated by his slaughter for it had been a formidable and glorious feat.

Of course. That was the solution. He realized that surrender was not needed. It took pride, and he was now laying himself bare with pride. He recalled a phrase from Freud who said that *the virtuous man contents himself with dreaming what the evil man accomplishes for real.*

He filled his lungs with air, jutting out his chest. He decided that it had not been a bad thing that that night he had decided to wear his worst faults, the darkest parts of his soul. And he had done so with the same grace that sometimes led the noble women of ancient Rome to worship the custom of walking around naked, wearing only their most lavish jewellery.

Still focused on his image he lowered his gaze slightly.

He noticed the vast patches of blood on his shirt and was thrown abruptly back into reality again, into that murky night.

He rearranged himself in the chair with his torso straight, clenched his fists and again displayed a haughty look, the look of the warrior. A new vigor seemed to take hold, once again, for that chained, proud and invincible looking man.

He believed that he had been granted the gratification of ascending to the God of death that fateful night. He had been given the power to judge, to condemn and finally to execute the death sentence.

This is what happens whenever a man surrenders to his demons.

But yet again his thoughts turned for a moment to reason, and he thought about what induced him to unleash his primal instincts. His sudden change had not been accidental, there had been a reason for it. That meek man had been turned into a monster, succumbing to survival, fear, anger, pain and pleasure.

"Pleasure," of course.

Observing his own dejected look in the mirror he finally realized that he had felt pleasure. A feeling of immense satisfaction, of final accomplishment.

"No one fully realizes themselves before they die," he thought.

Had he really become so blind, so incapable of reason? He remained motionless and pondered. NO!

He responded by speaking directly to his consciousness. He had not turned into a monster, he had only surrendered to the primitive rules of Mother Nature, released the rituals of the ancient gods and had let his primal nature gush forth without restraint.

Rationally and with absolute conviction he had decided to replace the Angel of Death. That night he had become Charon and had ferried the wretched into the cruelest circles of hell, who without a shadow of a doubt deserved that eternal punishment.

CHAPTER 10

The uphill road and the downhill road are the same road.

Heraclitus

Mark Alessi had thrown the murderer into a cell.

Usually catching delinquents gave him a certain feeling of complacency. When he succeeded in catching the worst ones he was moved by a sense of satisfaction. An ineffable feeling of enjoyment that resembled excitement.

But John Reginald Powell had turned himself in. No arrest. On the contrary, he had immediately and spontaneously confessed. It had taken all the adrenaline out of the case.

Except… that was not it… That could not be it.

If his state of impatience had depended only on the lack of excitement, he would have to consider himself nothing more than a sadistic vigilante.

He felt a certain inner turmoil, almost as if the weight of that night's tragedy had settled on his shoulders and had somehow chained him, suffocating him under a shadow whose nature he could not interpret.

His stomach had inexplicably tightened, and he had been enveloped in an undecipherable gloom.

Thinking of Reginald and of the tragedy of that night, he thought that there are greater misfortunes. Misfortunes capable of disturbing and transforming every perception, every emotion, of penetrating to the depths of truth.

"After all," he thought, "man thinks he is an evolved being, but he is just an animal with defective instincts carefully stored in the unconscious but untamed and alive. These are only kept at bay by the rules society imposes on us but they are ready to pounce at the first opportunity."

He turned on his car radio, without really listening to what it was broadcasting, and he left.

After the first few turns, however, a local station began broadcasting a Nick Drake song, *Northern sky.* That delicate and elegant piece rushed to his rescue. It soothed his burdened soul and restored some peace.

"There is not a glimmer of light missing even in the darkest of men," he thought again. He had seen that glimmer.

He had glimpsed in the man's eyes madness and reason coming head to head, each prevailing over the other in turn. In the contemptuous behavior of that seemingly sadistic man, there was from time to time a glimpse of brilliance which illuminated his presence.

He could not find an explanation, but he knew that there was something wrong with the night Powell decided to kill.

He realized that to solve this case he had to understand why, and had to delve into the darkness of the tragedy to discover what lurked within it.

He felt sure that he had crossed paths with one of the most terrible and evil of beings, capable of disemboweling a body without batting an eyelid, without feeling the slightest disgust, without feeling the weight of it on his conscience. He marveled when he realized that, in spite of everything, he could find true contempt for that man. On the contrary, he felt strongly that what he had before him was a person within whom madness coexisted with genius. All that unpleasantness was the price to be paid to allow such genius to survive.

Mark continued down the road, immersed in his thoughts that had a single anchor. John Reginald Powell.

He was home.

Sharon Flowers, the *Washington Post* reporter and his beautiful companion, was waiting for him. He had warned her with a text before he had left the department.

She had prepared the usual warm embrace.

He turned off the lights. The room was now illuminated by the Manhattan night, with its wavering lights and deceptive colors which filtered through the two large windows of his apartment on Furman Street. Sharon was sitting on the white leather sofa in front of the window. That was their favourite seat.

Sharon was a discreet woman. She had learned in life that caring too much drains a person, even if sincere, and this attitude allowed her to always be gentle and never intrusive.

She sat with her arm against the armrest and a glass of red wine in her hand. Her head rested lightly against the back of the couch, and a few strands of blond hair fell against the white backrest. She remained silent. She knew her loose hair, purposefully to attract Mark's attention, would manifest her presence.

After a while, however, she decided to lift her arm and greet him with a silent gesture. Mark took off his jacket, placed it on the back of a chair, filled his wine glass and walked slowly toward the sofa. He slumped wearily down beside that woman who had once stolen his heart.

He did not turn to look at her. He observed the Manhattan skyline and waited. For a moment he preferred to simply imagine her gorgeous face illuminated by the glow of the city that never sleeps.

She passed the wine glass to her other hand and raised it. Mark did the same. The glasses brushed against each other and emitted a quiet yet perfectly clear tinkling of crystal. So did their souls, gently touching and vibrating in the silence of their small world.

They both took a sip. Then she leaned her head on Mark's shoulder and watched a glittering Manhattan from above.

Mark moved his head in turn, brushing her hair with his ear. Sometimes their love knew how to be light and delicate, made up of warm silences, small nods imbued with feeling and understanding.

They knew how to connect in the silent and delicate world of small gestures.

But she could not resist for long. Slowly she turned and looked up at him. He closed his eyes, and gently rested his lips on hers.

A year earlier they had been taken in by the god Eros. They had loved each other physically, passionately making love. Soon, they had been overwhelmed by the most wonderful of ancestral laws, the one that transforms the love for a body into the love for a person.

The sky was clear and bright, dazzled by the glittering lights of New York City, rising up to the vault of heaven. A slice of the moon seemed to lie faintly on the tips of skyscrapers. It seemed to want to rest and doze there. Maybe even dream.

Mark's thoughts were alienated for a few moments. Yet the anguish of the day, which seemed to have vanished for a moment, came rushing back soon enough.

In the department's cell was the most vicious murderer that he had ever encountered. A monster who still seemed to have some kindness in his eyes. A man of mild demeanour, but with an impossibly fierce disposition.

His wandering attitudes confused him, his madness disturbed him.

Mark closed his eyes. He took a deep breath and took another sip of wine. He placed a light kiss on Sharon's blonde hair.

When he opened his eyes again he saw a single cloud, thin and white cutting the moon through its middle and expanding its white halo of light, scattering rays of opaline light into the surrounding sky.

As soft as cotton wool.

CHAPTER 11

Nature paints for us, day after day,
Images of infinite beauty

John Ruskin

The neon light suddenly grew darker and began to flicker. It kept turning on and off intermittently, typical behavior of an obsolete system that needs replacing.

The coming and going of light brought back a distinct memory for John Reginald Powell.

He looked up at the ceiling and stared at the ceiling light until he was blinded by it.

Instinctively he closed his eyes and an image appeared to him of that same flickering light now filtering through the leaves of the large trees under which he ran as a child. It alternated through areas of shade and areas where the sun could penetrate through the dense foliage.

The stuttering neon light catapulted his memory there, beneath the Louisiana trees, and it seemed to him, as he kept his eyelids tightly shut, identical to the alternating sunlight that he had seen so many times while running beneath the majestic, rich foliage.

In his world of memories he saw the sun piercing the green sea of leaves at times as if it were a giant light bulb, luminous and scorching, and remembered the shadowy areas caressing his warm skin with a cool, benevolent breath.

Yet, during his childhood Reginald was often too distracted to notice the subtleties.

He lived in a world made up of games, but was also overpowered by the desire to discover the wonders of the mystery of life. He wished to walk down its paths and to savor its emotions intensely, one by one, while breathing in all the sensations, especially those capable of shaking the tumultuous soul of a child who, completely unaware, is taking his first step into adolescence.

At that time he did not realize it at all. He was just a child, immersed in the vital commitments of a young boy: playing in cornfields, running in the shade of large trees, breathing the same warm, humid air as his friends, diving into the clouds of dust lifted by the great tractors, often in the company of a smiling Marion.

The memory of the sunlight piercing through the green foliage was only now resurfacing. It seemed to him that before this very moment the intermittent radiance had never existed. He had the impression that at that time there had been no sun, no light through the leaves.

Yet, there had been.

He simply had not noticed it. In those years, with childish naiveté, he had seen the sky without looking at it. He had scanned the vast, golden cornfields without realizing how wonderful and immense they truly were. For him it had been simply a place to play. A big playground stretching over acres and acres of land. An immense space of absolute freedom.

Now, thanks to a flashback, a clear and luminescent memory, he recognized and savored all the nuances, all the details, clear as day.

Reginald was realizing that he held within him wonderful memories that he had never truly processed. Like a fascinating book stowed away in a beautiful bookcase that, as wonderful as it could have been, had never been opened.

He now recalled one scene in particular, one that repeated itself every day when he came home. From a distance he could always hear his mother playing the piano.

It was a call.

The gentle sound of the piano reached over the surrounding plains and, in his recollections, now enveloped the whole of Louisiana, spreading through sensible souls, leaping from heart to heart, across America, across the world, eventually filling the whole universe. When he heard that sound, Reginald knew it was time. He would abandon whatever he was doing and head home through the cornfield.

In his memory he could see the image of his mother, in the room at the top of the stairs, sitting on the floor in front of the wide-open balcony. The light evening breeze made the white curtains sway toward her, touching her gently. She never stopped playing. With a simple gentle gesture, a slight lift of the chin and a smile, she gestured to a door behind which he would find a steaming bathtub ready for him.

His mother played an old piano that his father had received as a gift, a reward for a big favor rendered to a white man. A friend, one of the few white friends Papa Joseph had. No one had ever tried to ask what the favor was, but from that day on, his father had started thinking about moving to New York.

For many years Reginald had not opened the gate to his *garden of memories*. For many years his memory and imagination had merged into a sweeter version of his past. He realized however that he had not erased that file from his mind. The movie of his childhood had been shelved, hidden in a remote corner, but it was there. Indelible.

It was not clear to him for what reason he had pushed those memories to the side. Yet his eyes were again filled with visions of beauty, his heart was becoming serene again, and his soul still seemed able to rejoice.

With the images evoked by his memory he was finally succeeding in fully appreciating the wonders of his childhood. Those memories did not contain negative events at all; there was nothing sad, nothing gloomy. The resurfacing of those moments was as unexpected as it was wonderful, and the memories that emerged were as exciting and sweet as ever.

All but one.

There was one ugly, horrible event. It was to be traced back to the worst day of his life. A single day that his complacent mind suddenly threw up violently. That damn neon light should not have meddled. The rushing resurfacing of that day was now accompanied with a new dose of pain and torment. That cursed afternoon had played an important part in his life. And at that very moment he remembered why. They call it *forced memory*.

The memory resurfaced impetuously, the picture reassembled with all of its load of overbearingness and intimate devastation.

Surely it had to be because of that. He had removed a whole period of his life, the most significant, the most exciting, the most carefree, because of a single episode, a single day, a single dreadful afternoon.

He had been happy in Louisiana.

"We found him on the bench in the south side, right where you pointed us to." The visions were abruptly interrupted by Detective Brugger's brusque and jarring voice.

Powell detached from his memories and was catapulted back into the events of that night. He felt heavily disturbed. He had not finished sailing in the quiet and reassuring sea of his childhood. A sea that had then been taken by a storm. He had not been able to complete his course, to overcome the rough waters and find safety.

John Reginald Powell showed an increasingly icy indifference toward the massacre carried out that night. What did he care?

Nothing that had happened could scratch his callous armor of insensibility. Nothing would ever be able to etch a single scratch in his consciousness. No ugly scars would remain on his heart and none of the old ones would heal. At that moment he desired one thing: to return to the joyful memories. The volcano had erupted and dispersed the pain into the atmosphere. In an instant his greatest anguish was the bursting desire to be freed from the memories that had remained dormant for so long, segregated in a corner of his memory. They were now suffocating him.

He gritted his teeth, annoyed by the detective's highly inopportune intrusion. He only wished he could have continued to savor every moment of that bittersweet memory.

"The dead are dead," he thought. "Fuck them to hell."

He opened his icy red eyes and pinned Detective Brugger with a menacing gaze and for the first time the detective felt the weight of it.

Silvio remained motionless. That look had penetrated all the way into his heart. He wanted at all costs the cold shiver that went through him, a mixture of anger and fear running down his neck all the way down his spinal cord.

CHAPTER 12

Every day the lust for sin increases and shame decreases.

Lucius Anneus Seneca

e first heard a commotion. Footsteps, voices, noises. Then, a uniformed officer turned the corner of the hallway, approached the bars and locked the handcuffs on Powell's wrists. He opened the cell, grabbed Reginald roughly by the arm and led him once again to room 2. The interrogation room.

He waited a few minutes, illuminated by the stuttering neon light, until three policemen entered the room. Detectives Mark Alessi and Silvio Brugger, and Captain Bishop.

"We found him on the bench in the south side, right where you pointed us to."

There was a long minute of silence. All three of them stood and waited for Reginald to open his eyes again and return to the real world.

"So many police officers… I'm flattered," Powell said. He grinned contemptuously as he stared at his cuffed wrists.

"I don't know why, but I almost feel like a circus attraction right now. *Today, gentlemen and gentlemen, we're here in New York City for the monster shooooow... wooow... applause.*"

The sarcastic tone did not faze the officers. Everyone remained neutral, as if they expected such an act. After all, the questioned subject had the temperament of a psychopath, or something very close to it.

"You should at least pay me to see the show, don't you agree?" Powell accompanied the question by pushing his head forward, wide-eyed and wearing a derisive smile.

"Do you have any idea who you slaughtered, you idiot?" Captain Bishop immediately began pressing him. "You killed Jacob Madidoff, the eldest son of our governor's biggest campaign donor. A man who owns half of New York, publicly traded companies, hotels, restaurants…"

"Oh, come on, a Jew, a fucking Jew, ha ha. My God, detective. Are you telling me I should be afraid now?" John Reginald Powell lifted his gaze, smiling menacingly and staring straight into Simon Bishop's eyes.

He seemed to want to threaten the captain as well. He had a cocky air and eyes still hungry for evil.

The unkempt beard now appeared more wild, he became more and more tense, as did the mood of his hosts. Powell was summoning up the traits of a killer, the ruthless psychopath, his face was streaked with sweat, his jaws clenched and his nostrils flared.

"Hitler was just the tip of the Iceberg, you know Detective?" He spoke coldly.

"Captain. Call me Captain."

"Oh, my goodness. Captain, of course. Then I'll call you *Caaaaaptain*," he tried to lift and spread his arms wide to the sky, as if to address a prayer to a higher being. Halfway through, however, the movement was brusquely interrupted by the chains snapping with a cold metallic crack.

Powell paused to contemplate his arms rendered useless by the chains, his thick wrists locked in steel handcuffs. Breathing hard and open-mouthed, he gazed slowly at his right arm, then his left. He felt that his spirit, born free, was now caged within that department and realized that he would never find freedom again.

But how can one imprison a spirit, a soul, an essence?

He looked at himself in the mirror again. His soul seemed to rush inside that reflected image and become imprisoned in the mirror itself, as if an enchantment, or a curse, was gripping it, holding it hostage in a new world from which it would not return.

He came back to himself and adopted a serious tone. He shifted his posture to a normal stance and his expression changed abruptly to resemble a friend with whom one exchanges small talk at a bar.

And he resumed, "Do you seriously think that a fucking Negro, in this shitty country, can afford the luxury of being a racist towards a Jew? Do you really think that even if I wanted to, I could afford it? Ha, Ha, Ha... my God... *Caaaaptain.*"

He tapped lightly with his knuckles on the table as a fat, sarcastic laugh echoed within the interrogation room. Then Powell became suddenly serious again.

"You should study some history, Captain."

John Reginald Powell appeared capable of changing his attitude in an instant, from serious to sarcastic and back to serious. Then he started up again, mean and angry. "Emperor Hadrian spoke of the Jews as the slipperiest of peoples, capable of putting two things before everything else." He took a long pause. He began twisting his neck as if to release tension, to relax his jaw; he breathed in deeply through his nostrils. "Two things, two gods. Their God and their Money. For these two things they are even willing to sell their mother or brother."

"I have good news for you," Silvio Brugger interrupted him.

"We do not entertain anti-Semitism here and for us all beings have equal dignity."

"Beautiful sentiment, my dear Detective; almost encyclopedic, I would say. But one fact remains evident. The Jews have always gotten on everyone's nerves. The Romans, the Egyptians… they were mistreated in the Middle Ages. August Renoir, the great painter, also actively produced anti-Semitic propaganda. And what about Churchill and Stalin? They persecuted them too. Churchill sent thirty thousand to Hitler, did you know, my lovely Detective? The *Gulags*, Stalin's prison camps were on a par with the Nazi lagers. But they won the war and we don't speak ill of the victors, we are only allowed to speak ill of the atrocities committed by the losers."

Silvio placed his large hands on the table and brought his face closer until it almost touched Powell's sweat-soaked nose.

"I don't give a shit!" He had no desire to be taunted by that crude murderer, a psychopath who reeked of dried blood and sour sweat.

Powell did not flinch. On the contrary he sprung forward and hit, admittedly without much conviction, Brugger's forehead.

"I don't give a damned fuck either, Detective." he spoke under his breath, thin strands of drool spitting between his lips.

"I am not against Jews. I don't care about ethnic groups. I'm just pointing out that if they're on everyone's ass, well, there must be a reason. Maybe they're not all racist, maybe they're not all crazy. Maybe it's the Jews, who are greedy, slimy, fanatical, and God knows what else." He twisted his neck and curled his right lip as he spoke.

Mark Alessi grabbed Silvio by the arm and pulled him back.

"Now stop it, both of you." He said. "We are not here to put the Jewish people on trial, and we are not going to be the ones to pass judgement on whether the Jews are good or bad. Nor are we at all interested in your low opinion, if you must know." He brought his arms to his sides.

"So you didn't know he was Jewish? You didn't even know who he was, what his name was. So why on earth did you kill Madidoff?"

"I am not interested in Jews, I repeat. It was just a historical consideration. And anyway... if that piece of shit was called Madidoff... well... I confess. I'm happy twice over. But not because he was Jewish. Because he was a filthy rich, spoiled brat from upper class New York."

He opened icy eyes wide. He lifted the corners of his mouth and flashed yet another mocking grin, nasty and full of sarcasm. The detectives and the Captain looked at each other. Then, with a nod of momentary surrender, they left the room palpably disappointed.

When they reached the corridor, they huddled in a circle and examined each other's faces. Neither of them uttered a word for endless seconds. Each of them knew that they were unlikely to get anything useful out of that strange psychopathic man.

They agreed on only one thing. The most plausible lead seemed to be that of social revenge. For some reason, Powell had felt a desire to destroy the life of a young man, who's only fault seemed to be his wealthy family, and his carefree enjoyment of wealth.

Too carefree, at least in the mind of John Reginald Powell.

CHAPTER 13

I often find that I stare up at the stars on nights when they seem to throb with love.

Leonardo da Vinci

He was only a child at the time. But now he was there, sitting staring into a mirror that faded until it became a blank slate onto which someone was insistent on projecting the events of his life.

The gate to the *garden of memories* had opened wide again. The image and sensations he felt the first time he saw Manhattan had never disappeared from his mind but were now resurfacing with the powerful majesty of a whale emerging imposingly from the ocean.

They arrived in the evening, after a gruelling drive from Baton Rouge, in Papa Joseph's '68 Chrysler *Newport Town and Country*, faded beige in color with brown stripes streaked across the car doors.

The ugliest car in the world was, for him, the most beautiful car in the world. It was the perfect car for playing cops and robbers.

As a child, Reginald loved to climb over the back of the seat and jump inside the enormous trunk. He used to do this all the time. He even did it on that trip from Baton Rouge to New York.

He stretched out on his stomach, planted his elbows on the dusty carpeted bottom and looked out the rear window. On the road he imagined a large number of enemies. He pretended to be shooting at imaginary, villainous pursuers, armed to the teeth who exploded hundreds of rounds of ammunition but could not hit the target, just like in the best action movies. One shot splintered the edge of the bodywork and let off a silvery spark, another shot bounced off the ground, with jet sparks and small columns of smoke, then bouncing away to his left. Yet another near shot went by his right ear and was lost to the void. A few times his fervent imagination even let a bullet scrape by his arm. After a few intense grimaces of pain at how strong his imagination was, Reginald would sling on his machine gun and release all his anger, letting loose a bloody reaction capable of exterminating them all. One by one.

Papa Joseph did not like his son jumping back and forth from the seat to the trunk, but, after the first couple of hours, he had stopped scolding Reginald.

Of course, he would have liked his son to be quietly sitting next to him, in composed silence, perhaps engaging the time by talking about his mother, trying to fill the void in his heart by reminding him of how graceful, mild- mannered, and caring she was.

After a while, however, he realized that that *grecian cry* would do little good to a child's fragile mind. And little would it also benefit his adult psyche, still dazed by such an untimely death.

"Better to let him vent," he thought, "better to distract his fragile nature with childish and innocent games." Reginald had ended up falling asleep in the trunk, wedged into his last refuge, a trench between two suitcases where he had settled to hide from his terrible pursuers. He had settled on his left side, rested his thin leg on the top of the suitcase and his little head on the rear headrest of the seat.

Papa Joseph had been left looking at it as one looks at the last fragile bulwark that separates real life from clumsy survival. With love and with abandonment, but also hope, with the desire to go on, to start again, to dedicate himself fully to a new mission, to find a renewed purpose in some hidden recess of the soul.

It was there, before his shining eyes. A new mission. He slept serenely as if the world could not touch him.

The untouchable innocence of a child.

Joseph stretched out on the back seat and fell asleep; not without filling his eyes with the beautiful image of his son's face, smiling serenely in his sleep. The next day's journey had continued for more than twelve hours. When they stopped for lunch at a fast food diner, Reginald had jumped to attention, a strange behavior, unusual for him. There, in that unfamiliar little town, lost in some corner of America, there was not much difference between white men and black men. He had immediately noticed the light-skinned mixing with the dark-skinned without apparent problems. *Negroes,* as he habitually heard them called in Louisiana.

He had felt an unusual and very strange sensation when an elderly lady had passed her frail, trembling hand, rippled by time, on Reginald's curly head.

"What a beautiful child. What's your name, darling?" She had asked him.

Incredulous and pleased he had promptly responded: "John Reginald Powell, miss."

The elderly woman had smiled, her dry cheeks crinkling and showing all the years she had spent on this earth.

A smile full of life, an expression filled with tenderness that only those who now behold resignedly and serenely their own demise can bestow.

After getting back on the road and resuming the long journey, Joseph had driven until evening. From the window Reginald had seen the night fill the sky with an untold number of stars.

He had seen it a million times in Baton Rouge, but only now was he noticing the wonder of that black tapestry dotted with tiny yet impossibly bright specks.

He saw a shooting star and immediately thought that his mother was greeting him from up there. He raised his hand and silently returned the greeting.

"From up there I will always be watching you," she had told him. It was her, it could only be her. He was sure of that.

He stayed a few moments with his hand resting on the window and carefully scanned the sky, waiting for another affectionate sign of his mother's presence.

It did not come. That shooting star had filled little John Reginald's heart with a sense of tranquillity.

"Mother is still with me, watching me from heaven," he said to himself. "I knew it, she never lied to me, my mama." He let go with a final nod, his gaze skyward and his little hand still resting on the car window. The gesture was delicate, imperceptible.

Slowly the pitch blackness transformed; the sky was at first invaded by a kind of fragile whiteness. Then, slowly, it became veiled, white, expressionless.

At first in the distance, like a mist, a faint glow, then increasingly opaque, almost cloudy, to the point that the tapestry of stars disappeared completely.

Reginald thought back to full moon nights. Those times when the night became day, the Louisiana fields took on soft, soothing colors, and the silence expanded its blissful lightness to soothe even the most tumultuous of spirits. It seemed as if God himself was projecting down his divine aura, light of serenity and inner peace.

Suddenly, while he was deep in his thoughts mixed with memories, Papa Joseph grabbed his arm and gently pulled him closer.

Reginald turned and saw in the background an incredible silhouetted panorama.

The tallest buildings in the world projected their sumptuous light all the way to heaven. They illuminated the sky so brightly that Reginald became convinced that up there, in that sky, beyond that luminescent glow, resting on that blinding white mantle, was God, with his saints and winged angels.

The sky above New York City was heaven, and surely his mother was there too.

"Of course. Mother greeted me because she is here. My mom is in heaven."

Manhattan, with its twinkling lights, white and red and then again intermittent and shimmering and…. and…. He did not know what else to think, that child with a heart filled with wonder and excitement.

It looked like a huge amusement park. Or at least, that's how he saw it in his imagination.

He imagined himself running between merry-go-rounds, then aboard massive roller coasters, and on ass-kicking rides, whirling around and smiling with his gaze turned backward.

New York City was casting its thousand promises. Of happiness, of joy, of a new and hopeful beginning.

Soon, however, Reginald would discover that the twinkling lights of New York are like fireflies. They shine but do not warm.

They warm nothing at all.

CHAPTER 14

A question that leaves me confused. Am I crazy or are others crazy?

Albert Einstein

An officer rushed without knocking into interrogation room 2. "They found... *oufff... oufff...*," he gasped with great agitation, "...a body...." He continued by holding onto the door handle with one hand while holding onto the doorframe with the other. He had been running and his breath was labored, his voice shaky.

"In a Midtown hotel – a body lying on the ground. It appears to have been dismembered, practically torn to pieces. The responding officers say...," he drew in a lungful of air, "... they say he was most likely killed with an axe."

Ending with those grim words, he turned his head toward the man handcuffed to the suspect stand.

In a second he scrutinized him and condemned him.

The policeman was the same one who had received Powell at the entrance; he remembered him very well. Had he talked about massacre? No, perhaps not.

He had come in with his bloody contraption and had only asked to be arrested. From there, probably, his terror-filled imagination had constructed a massacre. He felt confused and sick, and the more he stared at the man, the more clearly he could see the image of a ruthless serial killer.

"He did it," the officer thought without saying a word. "It is undoubtedly his doing."

John Reginald Powell did not turn toward the officer at the door.

His face was stamped with a scornful, malicious expression, which exploded, in the short span of a couple of seconds, into a loud, caustic laugh.

"Ha, ha, ha, he's sure to be another fucking Jew, ha, ha," he announced with extreme sarcasm. Then he became serious and all his wickedness deflated.

"TELL ME HIS NAME, FOR GOD'S SAKE!" With a quick twist of his neck he nailed his contemptuous gaze into the eyes of the officer. He yanked his arms closer and pulled the chains tense. Instinctively he tried to wriggle free by struggling for a few seconds with his handcuffs.

God, if only his hands had been free.

He would have smashed that table, thrown the policeman right through the mirror, torn the door apart. He would have flown away like the wind, turned into a cloud in an endless sky. Ethereal. Impregnable.

A black cloud in a sky of white clouds. It would choose its victims from above, chase them down and kill them.

And then he would kill again and again.

Quite suddenly he placated his anger. Abruptly, as always happened. In a rush he would come and in a rush he would go.

He thought that, after all, he was the one who had showed up at the department; he was the one who had asked to be arrested.

"We don't know yet, dickhead," Mark Alessi approached him, placing both palms on the table.

"Why don't you try and tell us what his name was... After all you cut him up, you'll know who you killed ... or am I wrong?"

"Of course I do." Powell snapped forward and positioned his nose an inch from Alessi's face.

His nostrils flared again, his gaze grim with defiance; his pupils were dilated, anger oppressing his soul, bile rising all the way to his head.

The detective again smelled the stench of blood and sweat.

He resisted for a moment. Then he recognized the thick smell of evil, of rage, of spite as it pervaded his body completely.

Abruptly he pulled back.

Sometimes wickedness can be contagious. It passes from a corrupt soul to an uncertain soul and allows the latter to be defiled by imitation, following the former down into the abyss.

Alessi knew this very well. He knew that sort of metempsychosis that makes a soul, a feeling, a sensation, migrate from one body to another.

He had felt it every time he had arrested a killer, a pedophile, or a rapist. The temptation to kill them, to take them out there and then had been great.

The desire for revenge, for rough justice had always arisen for him. It would pervade his whole body, from the legs, to the heart, to the mind.

The law that is lost in the mists of time. An *eye for an eye, a tooth for a tooth.*

Like a tidal wave, the rage had transcended and broken his spirit. At certain moments he would have wanted to murder the murderer, slaughter the slaughterer, rape the rapist, torture the pedophile.

He had always been rescued by reason, holding him back andand bringing the primal instincts back into their enclosure. *Refrain, O humans, from defiling the body*, says Pythagoras in a work by Ovid, *The Metamorphoses*. The poet in his work refers to food, but Mark Alessi had adapted that concept to his instinctive and sometimes sanguine nature. "This is a job that has to be done with detachment," he repeated often to himself, "never let the soul be contaminated."

"Another fucking asshole, that's who I killed..." Powell pulled back, resting his massive body back against the chair.

"... Maybe Jewish, maybe Chinese, maybe American… Who's to tell?" he lowered his gaze and stared AT some conspicuous blood stains on his pants.

He remembered vividly the boy killed in the room at the Planetarium Hotel. He had followed him down the street. He had seen him get out of his car with the swagger typical of youth. He was handsome, elegant, and smiling. Under his three-quarter-length coat he had noted a lean, well-proportioned physique. A model's physique.

Powell had seen him enter the hotel lobby just as the warm night was going through its darkest hours. Taking advantage of the semi-darkness and sparse staff in the lobby, John Reginald had sneaked in and followed the boy to his room.

Yes, the bloodstains on his right leg were from the man in the hotel.

He had entered the room slowly and quietly passed in front of a mirror near the entrance. His pants, in the reflected image, were still the typical light blue color of jeans.

He was certain. It was the boy's blood that he was now staring at. He remembered perfectly every single blow, each slash hurled with extreme violence as panic flashed on the boy's face, which became a grimace of horror and gasps of terror. And the terror mixed with pain and the pain numbed, losing its intensity, and became resignation, until life finally dissolved.

A face that looked as if it were asleep were it not for the drops of blood that spotted across it like freckles .

He had witnessed each change in his facial features. First the rapid contraction of horror and then the slow, passive relaxation as he surrendered to death. Powell had stood still and watched the life drain rapidly from his eyes, accompanying it with a sense of fulfilment and satisfaction.

In John Reginald Powell, anger seemed to recoil and take flight, quickly. He was capable of rapid mood swings and extreme emotional digressions.

He looked at his hands and recognized the instruments of torture, the weapons with which he had made such a definitive gesture, that had tugged or snatched joyful lives from those young boys.

They could have graduated, raised a family, had a decent job, perhaps become successful managers.

When he thought of death, John Reginald Powell also imagined that mysterious, unknown world accessed through it.

He was ignorant, like every man, of what happens beyond that dark door, but the Christian faith that he had been indoctrinated into in childhood and that had occupied his spirit in adolescence had always allowed him to fantasize about the existence of a heaven, a purgatory and a hell.

He kept telling himself that *if everyone goes, surely it must not be so terrible.*

Although he had recently turned fifty, he still firmly believed that first his mother, and then his father, had been welcomed by the Good Lord into the Kingdom of Heaven.

Silvio Brugger noticed Powell's blank stare and realized that he was completely immersed in his thoughts. Without anger, without hatred. He was simply immersed, serene or at the very least relaxed.

"So, Powell...," these two short words, whispered almost under his breath by Detective Brugger, were enough to suddenly tug at the killer's conscience.

In his mind flooded with madness, hatred and rage resonated with the roar of a storm, an inner voice, a certainty; *those pieces of shit must all croak in hell.*

Even God, from up there, even his beloved mother, from heaven, would have approved of his actions.

That was his path. That was his last mission.

CHAPTER 15

True havens are the havens we have lost.

Marcel Proust

They had arrived in New York City and settled into an apartment on the twelfth floor of a decidedly run down building. It was dilapidated, of an anonymous gray color, held up only by filth and dust, the stairs invaded by a musty, acrid, pungent smell. The entrance, hallways and landings were completely defaced with scribbles and squalid graffiti.

One could frequently hear people yelling, arguing or making love, but could never tell from which apartment of that crowded pigeon coop the sounds were coming.

There were no neighbors and no encounters except unwanted ones. No family, no tenant in that building would have dared to put their noses outside the door even if they heard the fire alarms howling. Alarms which were obviously absent in that building.

You had to stay away from those people, not try and get friendly with anyone; in short, mind your own business.

"Surely, good people must be here also," little Reginald had thought.

But Joseph had heard many bad stories, too many tales of thugs, prostitutes, drug dealers, vicious fights, drunk and violent fathers. Surely those tales belonged only to a small fraction of the tenants in the neighborhood, but Papa Joseph had nonetheless decided it would be better not to trust anyone. At the cost of becoming an overbearing parent.

It was precisely because of his father's stories that Reginald began to experience a strong feeling of unease, almost fear, whenever he walked through the front door of the apartment block.

He hoped the elevator would always work. He was not worried about getting tired; he was a strong and vigorous child capable of jumping the steps two by two up all twelve storeys. But when the elevator wouldn't work he was seized by a real fear of going up the stairs, because he knew he had to do so without glancing into those fetid, twilight hallways where he often happened to catch a glimpse of someone drunk in their underwear, clandestine couples tumbling against the walls or young boys exchanging conspicuous handshakes and dollar bills.

Except on the floor where a Chinese family lived. The eighth floor was occupied by a family that had arrived many years earlier from Hong Kong. There were so many of them that he couldn't keep count, but they were so discreet that he often doubted that they were there. There, on the eighth floor, all was silent, the chaos disappeared.

"They are discreet and quiet people," Reginald always thought each time he passed the eighth floor. "Just good people."

Sometimes the elevator would not want to work. Not because it would break down but because some of the tenants would use it without any sense of respect.

On the little red light, instead of *busy* they should have written: *I am sick and tired of carrying this uncivilized bunch up and down. Leave me alone.*

Though too long a sentiment to be expressed with a small red light, Reginald had often fantasized that it was the elevator itself that decided to stop working in protest.

There were those who stuck their chewing gum on the keys, those who farted in it, and those who vomited in it after a night of heavy drinking. Most of the time one could smell piss, other times the piss was still there, pooled on the linoleum floor.

When the elevator was stationary, however, it meant that someone had left the doors ajar, or perhaps left them open on purpose.

Up on the twelfth floor, little John Reginald Powell would enter the apartment, and there behind closed doors he would find some well-earned peace of mind. His fears dissipated. He felt safe inside his own fortress.

Yes, the fortress. It looked more like a prison than a fortress. Most of the time he was alone. He waited anxiously for his father to come home from work with some anxiety. He needed company and someone to talk to.

From the window he could only see the wall of the building opposite, made of bricks that once must have been red and had now taken on a dark, smoky gray, broken by tiny windows shielded by some more and some less colorful curtains allowing a glimpse of the life that went on inside those apartments. The street Powell lived on was all but an alley; a narrow, smelly alley, good only for housing trash and a few stray cats looking for food.

He missed his Louisiana days.

At night he often woke up smiling because in his dreams he could still feel the wind caressing his cheeks, see the fields of tall, lush corn again, and hear distinctly the sound of large tractors in the distance. They were approaching loudly as they do every year at this time. *Vroom. Vroom.*

Then he woke up and realized that the noise was garbage trucks emptying the bins outside.

His smile faded and he would stare at the ceiling where his happy memories were projected, like on movie screen, and he would immerse himself in his childhood in his Baton Rouge, his Louisiana.

There, where he could at least go out, where he could run in the meadows, breathe clean air and meet his friends.

There, in Baton Rouge, he had the space to be alive.

In Louisiana he could absorb every moment of freedom, indulge in his carefree childhood, enjoy every single and simple moment of happiness to the fullest.

The house where he lived with his family was not much, little more than a shack, masterfully repainted by his father ivory-white and made cozy by his mother's extraordinary care for small things.

The flowers, the ornaments, the paintings. Everything was in the right place. And the piano.

Reginald heard it from afar, every evening. On the Great Tractor Road on his way home at sunset, he would hear the sweet sound of his mother's beloved instrument. He could almost see those notes hover lightly in the air heedless of gravity. He could see them skimming the ground and caressing the trees, gently cradling the flight of birds and accompanying the sun to dip below the horizon, carried gently by the music and the soft breeze. When he arrived home his mother would not stop playing, not right away. She would wait for him to finish bathing then she would also call his father and start setting the table for dinner.

One evening, as he returned home through the fields he was seized by a feeling of emptiness. He realized that the emptiness was the lack of something he had taken for granted his whole life.

There was no sound, he did not hear the sweet flow of piano notes. And at the exact moment he realized it was not there he also realized, within himself, how crucial it was. With a kind of premonition, he began to run as fast as he ever had. He waved his arms frantically in front of his face to separate the leaves of the tall corn plants with his hands as he ran across the field. He wanted to be faster than the wind, faster than the tractors, faster than that terrible premonition.

The broad, sharp leaves of the corn plants that day decided it was worth being gentle. They stopped being sharp and seemed for a moment to want to caress the fidgety hands and wet face of that small child who was used to playing happily amongst them.

His tears, driven by the wind, had slid backward toward his ears and had traced two bright silvery trails that shone in the last lights of the sun as it fell behind the horizon.

Reginald had found himself on the lawn surrounding the house and stopped suddenly. He had watched his house for a second. He had stared at it while the lawn and surrounding fields seemed to become liquid, undefined, blurred.

The air had stopped, the silence had become surreal, everything was muffled; in that corner of Louisiana, the world seemed to have shut down.

Then he started running again, he crossed the lawn in a brief yet endless moment, entered the house, taking the stairs two by two and reached his parents' bedroom. He had stopped at the door and observed his mother lying down, covered in a white veil.

At first it seemed to him that she was sleeping deeply, for what little he could glimpse through the sheer cloth.

Her face was serene, as he had not seen it in months, completely relaxed. For a moment he had felt relieved, his mother's suffering face had vanished. His dear mother had found peace again.

But that moment had been very short-lived. He had suddenly felt a deep emptiness. Realizing that he would never see her again sitting on his floor, that he would never again enjoy her kind smile, that she would never again kiss his forehead before going to sleep, had plunged him into an abyss of grief.

And he had felt mocked.

How come no one had told him anything? Why had they kept him in the dark about his mother's illness?

Now he began to understand. The sickness, the ill-concealed suffering on her kind face, her body becoming more wispy, week by week.

The stubbornness with which his father had sought that instrument, his mother's incessant desire to play the piano to estrange herself, to shut herself away in her own world and not think about the illness that would soon snatch her from life. John Reginald had run away. He had gone down into the backyard and picked up a stick on the ground and started slashing it violently against the fence. One shot, two shots, a hundred shots. He screamed. Screamed so much that the world around him had stopped spinning.

The birds settled on the highest branches had stopped singing. The breeze stopped, the fluttering leaves quieted, the soft swish of the wheat stilled. This is how the universe had decided to respect his immense sorrow; in humble silence.

His father had heard his cry of anger and immense heartbreak. He had run down the stairs. Reginald was in the garden waving his stick in the air, beating the fence, the ground. Papa Joseph had ducked away from a couple of blows, and had then grabbed the bat and flung it away and wrapped his strong arms around his son while he was still flailing in torment.

They had wept together into the evening, locked in an embrace and united by grief.

Heavily within him, Reginald felt like he was going mad.

CHAPTER 16

The enemy to be defeated is not the other: it is ourselves.

Lancelot of the Lake

" $\mathcal{H}$ e never thinks about the victims. It seems that the unfortunate souls don't really exist in his mind. He doesn't talk about them and he doesn't want to hear about them."

"He doesn't care, it's all too clear. He didn't even know who they were... He shouted it in our faces. He didn't know his victims. Personally I think he is completely blinded by his madness."

Mark Alessi and Silvio Brugger were on their way to the hotel where the second body had been found. They sat in the car, Mark driving and Silvio in the passenger seat. Detective Silvio Brugger was holding his phone and trying to figure out, with Google Maps, which route had the least traffic.

"I noticed it from the start. His narrative is totally cold, his emotional participation is nil. What little he is throwing out is just anger, more or less mixed with folly. And, above all, he shows no sense of guilt."

Indeed, John Reginald Powell's behavior had been, up to that point, comparable to a fire that feeds on what it devours. When a flame envelops its prey, it engulfs it and uses it to feed itself.   Thus Powell fed anger with anger, madness with madness, contempt with contempt. But also calm, a seeming serenity that would sometimes arise and send the detectives into confusion.

"He doesn't seem at all distressed by what he's done, by all the atrocities he's committed with that fucking axe. When he's not exploding into angry episodes, the only thing he can show is that ridiculous grin. I have an urge– an urge to smash his fucking face in. He's a psychopath, I tell you. What do they call them? Subjects with severe personality disorders?"

"Something like that," Mark replied with an edge of indolence. He continued to hold the steering wheel with his left hand while with his right he stroked his goatee and surrounding 5 o'clock shadow.

"He goes from extreme anger to complete calm too easily. This is not normal behavior. It's fake, constructed, it might as well be an act– yeah, a fucking act. Either that guy really knows his stuff or we are dealing with a mind completely quashed by instincts; it has its moments of pure madness and then goes back to normal... if we can even talk about normality." He drew in his breath and looked distractedly out the window.

Silvio pulled a pack of cigarettes out of his pocket. He took one out and put it in his mouth without lighting it. He held it tightly between his lips. He was trying to quit smoking, but without suffering from abstinence, and not lighting the cigarette seemed like a good strategy to him.

Soon after, however, he took the cigarette back between his fingers and spoke.

"I think there is something that unnerves him. We know that he didn't know the two boys. Or that's what he wants us to believe. So he must have met them casually, he must have noticed things in those boys that he didn't like, I don't know – maybe they were smoking weed or drinking or being obnoxious – who knows. At that point, he certainly felt impulses of uncontrollable anger that caused him to slaughter them with his axe. Who knows what his psychopathic mind sensed... Yeah, I mean... You know what I mean, right?"

"Yeah, sure... Someone who suffers from fits of rage but goes around with an axe? I'm not so sure about that. I think he prepared before the attacks. At the very least he had to get hold of the weapon. And where did he get it? Was it his own? Who gave it to him? We still have to have a lot of questions answered, Silvio. And we also need to figure out a motive. Without a motive any jury would have a much harder time convicting him. They would still convict him, sure, but with insanity he would be reduced to a few years in a fucking mental hospital. He'd get ten years, serve five, and we'd be back to square one."

Mark had laid down a theory that seemed to make sense to his colleague. He seemed distracted, but had in fact been following Silvio closely while focusing on trying to interpret the killer's deeper psychology.

He had always been attracted to the emotions and deliberations that the mind is capable of generating. The brain, the organ that comes closest to the concept of perfection than anything else in the world.

When it works.

But the brain is also the most inscrutable organ, the most impenetrable. That is why every human being always remains a mystery to others. Even with a very close person, a relative, a friend, we will never fully grasp all their thoughts, the sensitivity of their soul, the charge of their deepest trepidations.

The brain, where everyone parks their deepest emotions, especially the unspeakable ones.

At his colleague's words, Silvio Brugger clenched his fists without even realizing it, in an almost entirely involuntary gesture. He gave one more fleeting glance, turning to the window again. Then, with a snap, he turned back toward his friend.

"Mark, you're right, he won't get off so lightly. We have to get him to confess at all costs, because I think if he doesn't confess ... it's going to be very difficult, almost impossible to make him pay for it completely."

He paused to reflect for a few more seconds. Mark did not say a word. He seemed focused on driving. He actually wanted to get there quickly, and at that very moment he felt strongly tempted to turn on the flashing lights and siren to push through at least some of that cumbersome traffic.

Silvio resumed, "It is crucial to get him to talk, it is necessary to draw everything out, it is vital that we convince him that telling the whole story can help him not only to get some leniency from the prosecutor but above all to release his conscience and relieve his remorse, assuming he has any. He has something undefined in him. And I think we have to push him for a confession by hitting the right chords, and help him open up in some way."

"I got it, I got it. We have to make him confess. You've repeated it a thousand times, Silvio. And we have to do it nicely. Of course– it's clear, it's not like we can torture him. So, let's consider for a moment the psychological state of someone who leaves the house with an axe."

Mark seemed to wake up suddenly. "We know that in almost all cases the one who tortures is not a man who has lived a normal life. On the contrary, only those who have been tortured, or even just repeatedly mistreated, become torturers themselves."

"I would not be so sure that Powell intended to torture his victims, Mark." Silvio immediately countered his misgivings. "To me it looks more like fits of rage, it looks to me like a short-circuit of the brain, a tranquil man who has been struck by the disease of violence for a reason he cannot explain or recognise, which looks very much like the germ of homicidal madness, a kind of delusional schizophrenia. He sees something nonexistent. He hears voices in his head that do not actually exist."

He turned his gaze toward his colleague and remained absorbed for a few seconds.

"Psychiatrists call it a *trigger* if I'm not mistaken. An event that suddenly resurfaces old trauma, I don't know... abuse, mistreatment, rape... in short, the bad things that the mind has been struggling to hide in a corner and unexpectedly resurface with their load of madness." He paused. "But it's just my feeling," he added.

"You're right, Silvio, when you say that he must have seen something or someone perform actions inappropriate to his personal code of behavior. Let's call it a trigger if you like. This caused a short circuit in his brain and the subsequent outburst of homicidal rage. But, as you also mentioned, these behaviors are usually consequences of trauma. Trauma creates a state of dissociation of consciousness similar to a hypnotic state. In this dissociative state there is room for autosuggestion."

"Autosuggestion, sure. He sees things that seem normal to all of us but to him evoke memories, related perhaps to episodes of mistreatment suffered during childhood or adolescence. These memories trigger disproportionately violent reactions. I agree. On that we agree. But what did he suffer through? And what led him to these two boys specifically?"

Detective Brugger wanted the case to be solved in all its facets, with no gray areas, no parts forgotten or unexamined.

Mark was often more hasty.

"The boys were simply in his path. They were in the wrong place at the wrong time. When people talk about fate… otherwise you're right. I know you're right, Silvio. Crimes need to be cleared up in their entirety, to not betray the expectations of the victims' families, of society, and most importantly, not allow other people, perhaps marginally involved but just as guilty, to get away with it. Sometimes though, I can't help but wonder what good it might do. Did he confess? Yes. Okay, then let's lock him up and let the judge and prosecutor deal with it."

"Sure. But we still don't even know how many he killed. What if there are more? How and where do we find other possible victims? The only solution is to continue to push him to confess everything, including his motive."

"A psychopath doesn't need a motive, it's not necessary, he doesn't need it. But have you seen him? He seems intoxicated by his exploits. When he talks about the victims he doesn't seem to be referring to kids, to human lives, to people with families, with affections, friends, relatives, with plans, with a life ahead of them. He seems to be referring to them as if they were punching bags. Stuff that you can even... why not... have a go at with an axe; it's all the same to him."

Mark seemed to want to metabolize it more philosophically, as if what happened could be fit into some kind of normality, as if the world could somehow accept that, from time to time, someone's mind can short-circuit and vent anger and frustration by unleashing violence, slaughtering people and killing innocents.

The history of mankind is full of stories of serial killers, psychopaths, rapists, and thugs of all kinds. He would not be the first, nor the last.

Detective Mark Alessi seemed to be reflecting on all this. Of course, that was not it. Not at all. After just one day that case already reeked of trouble. It had the hallmarks of front-page news, of a case that all of America would be talking about.

The Axe Serial Killer, the newspapers would headline; like a Stephen King novel, a new crime TV series or something of that sort.

On the contrary, handing over the murderous madman to justice immediately would mean silencing the whole media circus.

Which is no small thing.

"Let's see who the second murdered person is. We have to establish whether there is a connection between the two victims. Then we'll just have to figure out how both are connected to Powell, to his past, to his... fucking trauma."

Detective Brugger hinted that they should abandon all the psychiatry bullshit. Let psychoanalysts and psychiatrists have their way with investigating sick minds. They were cops, pragmatists, field actors looking for pieces of evidence to nail the bastards.

At least for the moment it was necessary to shoot straight. No behavioral paranoia, no bullshit, no psychosis theories. Evidence. It would take hard fucking evidence to finally dismiss the case.

Suddenly Mark Alessi turned on his flashing lights and parked the car. Silvio looked out the window and lifted his gaze skyward to read the hotel sign:

PLANETARIUM HOTEL.

They entered and looked around. The lobby had been cleared and the hotel guests diverted to a side exit, usually reserved for service personnel.

A pair of uniformed officers were standing guard just behind the sliding door to the entrance.

Mark and Silvio flashed their badges, and the officers nodded.

Silvio went straight to the reception desk and pulled out his notepad.

The boy at the desk had a composed and precise air to him. He stood stiffly, with upright posture like a stick planted in the ground and arms crossed behind him. On the breast pocket of his jacket was a label with the name "Dwayne."

"Hello Dwayne. I guess you already know what I want to know, right?"

"Good morning, Detective," the boy replied in a slightly tremulous voice. "Phil Grant, his name is Phil Grant. We know him well, he's a regular. He lives in Newark and when it gets late at night he stays over. Especially on weekends."

Silvio looked at him with a sad smile.

"You're right," the boy added softly, "...we *knew* him... sure, I understand. I should be using the past tense by now."

Heaven exists and it is this Earth of ours. But there is also Hell, and it consists of not realizing that we live in a paradise.

Paracelsus

Mark and Silvio gathered for an evening out with friends at the Village. *Wine Temptation* was a nice little place. Good wine, simple but good food. It was warm and cosy, and had a family friendly atmosphere.

The venue often had live music performances with somewhat improvised bands, but they were always good musicians and the tunes were pleasant to listen to.

That evening there was an almost all-female quartet that was reminiscent of the *4 Non Blondes*, the pop-rock group from which, in all likelihood, that evening's band had taken inspiration.

The singer wore a flashy top hat with a pair of 1930s aviator glasses placed above the brim. She had on a long purple-red velvet jacket and a pair of short shorts over faux leather ankle boots. With that attire, it seemed a throwback from the early 1990s. Even her facial features were a lot like Linda Perry, the vocalist of the Californian group. The girl held her guitar with the same unkempt style, she seemed almost bored. Swaying gracefully on her slightly bent knees she clasped the pick between her fingers and started with a *G major* as she gave the drummer, the only male member of the group, the signal to start. They began with *What's Up*, the most successful song. It was not a proper cover band, mostly because it was impossible. The *4 Non Blondes* had produced only one album in their short history. Too short.

And indeed, when the first song was over, the girl stripped off her velvet coat, removed her hat, and began jumping with disruptive energy to the notes of The Cranberries' *Zombies*.

Mark Alessi was chatting quietly with Sharon and their friends, drinking fine red wine, but always keeping an ear tuned to the music. Pop-rock that had its roots in the 1980s and 1990s represented a true musical passion for him. He listened to it all the time. He had dozens and dozens of old vinyl records, hundreds of CDs and downloaded tracks on his iPhone. With Sharon, they had decided that this would be an evening of pure and utter distraction. Away from work and from all that stress. Only laughter, friends and a good time. And that is exactly how it went. At least up to a certain point.

Silvio Brugger met Geena, Sharon's friend. She was gorgeous. She had curly hair and an intriguing smile. Her smile was shy and evasive, as she would duck her head whenever she laughed, letting her thick hair fall in front of her face and hiding the expression of joy behind a veil of hair, as if laughter were shameful.

Shy, thought Silvio, who, however, could not help but be intrigued by those imperfect gestures, those motions that unconsciously wanted to interpose distance but often achieved the opposite effect, namely that of inspiring empathy, a desire and curiosity to investigate thoroughly to try to understand behind what curtain of the soul Geena went to hide her laughter and sweet smile.

Mark noticed that the two had wandered away from the group to get a drink at the bar. He observed the scene from afar. He watched them and waited for contact. He waited for his hand to approach her naturally, without any malice.

He knew his friend was interested; maybe he would just speak into her ear with the excuse of the loud music. Or he would rest a hand gently and unassumingly on her arm. The most overt gesture he could have made would have been to take her hand. Too risky for the reserve that characterized both of them.

Mark Alessi was certain of this because he had over time learned his friend's behaviors. Human beings have a knowledge system based on emotion, and the highest degree of emotional connection is unquestionably achieved through touch.

Each of the five senses is capable of triggering strong feelings, but touch... touching someone... has a much deeper effect than all other senses. It is necessary to touch each other, even just to brush against each other for an instant, in order to bring forth that spark of empathy, a connection to another's soul.

The two were laughing, toasting, and drinking. Then, all of a sudden, Silvio had left the glass and raised his arm, placing his hand on Geena's shoulder. He kept it there for a few seconds, waiting for a reaction from her.

Then, instinctively, he had decided to dare. Inconspicuously perhaps, without even realizing it, Silvio timidly lifted his thumb upward in an attempt to caress her cheek with the elegant nonchalance with which a dragonfly rests on the petal of a flower on a riverbank.

She understood perfectly, bowed her head to an imperceptible degree, smiled with tenuous complicity, and met Silvio's simple, affectionate touch that had no other purpose than to reveal his emotional state, a suggestion of involvement and reciprocity.

They barely touched each other, thumb against cheek. That spontaneous and sincere gesture showed through their shining eyes, and they could not help but stare intensely at each other.

A sense of beauty spread through their hearts and bodies, and seemed to invade the entire space. Nothing of it was definitive, nothing ascertained; there were only small, intoxicating quivers of the soul.

And to tell the truth, neither of them wondered what on earth was going on. They enjoyed the interference of the spirit and felt those vibrations, wanting them to last as long as possible. Without any other purpose, without any behind-the-scenes.

Then that magical moment was interrupted at its peak, just as it happens in the best dreams. The phone rang.

Smartphones. Damned contraptions that are indispensible today. Technology that represents joy and pain. We let our phone become the container of our entire life: numbers, connections with the world, valuable information; and memories, friends, and the operation of home or office appliances. Without realizing it, we allow it to eventually encompass our lives. Most of us take our brains and decide, in total autonomy and without a second thought, to enclose them in a metal box with a touch screen and a camera.

The caller was an FBI colleague.

Silvio listened to him speak for a few endless moments, his eyes fixed on Geena's face with a blank stare and an incredulous expression.

Then he closed his eyes, drew in a deep breath and kept listening; the incredulous face turned into a white and inanimate stare, a marble-like expression.

In front of him Geena immediately grasped the gravity of the news Silvio was receiving. I was clear by now that the evening had been clouded, disturbed; that the carefree mood of the detective had sunk into a pit of anguish.

Brugger ended the call but continued staring at the screen as it went black.

At Grand Army Plaza, at the southeast corner of Central Park, the small body of an eleven, maybe twelve year old child had been found.

Abused, probably raped and then killed.

Silvio Brugger was still motionless, sunk in a state of disquiet, his eyes petrified and his breath held. He could still hear the echo of his colleague's voice in his mind.

They found a little girl. She was tortured. She died. They found a little girl. She was abused. She died. He lowered his hand slowly, kept his gaze fixed in the void and he slid down from the stool by the counter. On his face the oppressive anguish became visible to all.

Solid and icy.

He turned toward Mark Alessi. His colleague seemed to have perceived the negativity in the air and turned sharply to meet Silvio's gaze. The two had known each other since childhood and there was no need for words.

Not under those terrible circumstances.

Mark's face became a copy of his colleague's. He still had no idea what had happened, but he distinctly sensed tragedy.

Silvio turned to look at Geena. She too was shocked and felt her soul heavy with anguish. Silvio had not told her. She had heard.

"A child, My God!" were the only words Geena managed to utter as she covered her nose and mouth in shock.

With the one thin thread of voice, the detective whispered words he never wanted to utter to her, "I'm sorry, I have to go."

CHAPTER 18

What we know about ourselves is only a small part of what we really are outwith our knowledge.

Luigi Pirandello

*P*owell sat in his cell at the department and held his head in his hands, his elbows resting on his knees. From there he could hear almost everything.

He listened with a kind of detached interest. He picked up distinctly all the noises in the department but his was a state of confusion. That magma of muffled and clear noises, loud and barely perceptible, subtle rustling and deafening ring of telephones, voices, footsteps, agents, doors slamming, people demanding, suspects shouting their extraneousness to the facts, chairs scraping the floor.

My God!

Powell's brain was exploding in an attempt to elaborate, to make order while being continuously bombarded with the din of that stormy and chaotic place.

His mind was trying to disentangle itself in that narrow space, suffocated by claustrophobia.

At the same time, he was being lulled in the lap of sweet childhood memories to which he clung tenaciously and that continued to sustain him by bringing up feelings and thoughts that softened and confused everything. A mixture of reality and fantasy, of memories and imagination, of delightful circumstances and murky events. He could estrange himself in the fullness of those emotions and become serene again, if only for a few moments. Then the latest events and the silhouette of the axe again materialized in the horror in his thoughts, while on his face re-emerged, renewed and brutal, expressions of anger, ferocity and restlessness.

The story of Powell's spontaneous surrender had already circulated throughout the department; yet no one dared to talk about it to outsiders. The news had not yet been fed to the press for confidentiality reasons during the investigations, and the order not to breathe a word had been categorical.

Mark Alessi and Silvio Brugger were in the briefing room with Captain Simon Bishop and at least half a dozen other detectives and officers.

Powell's murders had not been the only ominous events to bloody the streets of New York City in recent times. Quite the opposite. During the last week, in particular, it seemed as if Lucifer himself had decided to ascend the circles of Hell with wide strides and show all of America just how much evil mankind is capable of.

Captain Bishop had the thankless task of managing all the work. Covering the new cases that were being added to old unsolved cases, that were being added to the even older and colder ones. Each one seemed to have top priority. For each of the crimes there was a section of the press ready to bite, for each crime a plethora of journalists, relatives and onlookers with a lust to investigate, to know, to write.

The pressure was the same as always; they were used to it. In New York City, the FBI flanks the police seamlessly. Statistics speak of nearly a murder a day in the economic capital of the States, but these almost never occur in the heart of Manhattan.

John Reginald Powell could glimpse from his cell a large screen tuned to CNN. It was placed at the end of a room whose door always remained open. The background noise did not allow him to hear the news; he was able however to discreetly distinguish the large print subtitles.

He stared at the monitor in the hopes of understanding, of dispelling the doubts that invaded his mind. He waited anxiously for the succession of news reports to somehow reveal the road his madness had travelled, the path of his heinous cruelty. His mind was desperately removing every memory of the previous night.

Time helps to erase everything, but how far back in time does an event have to be in order to be totally expunged?

Certainly Powell, only twenty-four hours later, was not on the road to oblivion. Not yet. He was painfully aware of all the evil he had committed, but his mental capacity had become opaque, and his reasoning was shuffling the cards, bringing a great deal of confusion; memories appeared disordered, distorted, haphazard.

"The defenses of the intellect," Reginald thought in a single moment of pure lucidity, a pause from that hysterical madness, an instant in which he managed to relax his muscles and lean his back and head against the wall with his arms crossed over his thighs.

He sensed the void that comes after a traumatic event, a void that removes and confuses.

He thought back to a book by Mark Twain in which the writer recounted seeing a man approaching along the driveway of his house. This man had then disappeared, only to reappear moments later inside the home.

The narrator had thought of magic or an illusionist's trick. Soon after, however, he had realized simply that his mind had become alienated from reality.

Mark Twain was so immersed in his thoughts that he could not even remotely perceive the presence of the person who had passed just a few feet from him and entered the house by knocking vigorously on the door.

Following a similar mechanism, Reginald knew that he had totally set aside the events, as if his body had acted autonomously, as if he had never been there, and even if he had been there... Well, he was not present to himself.

It was perhaps what they call *false memory syndrome.*

It happens when you confuse the fruits of your imagination with reality; it often happens after a traumatic event.

But John Reginald Powell knew that sooner or later the memories would return, that he would recall everything clearly, lucidly, and consciously. He was not crazy; he had never been crazy. Or at least he had never noticed it, never sensed it. He had never faced such a mental short circuit. He was sure of that. He would have known it. He would have remembered it.

He grasped his head in his hands and shook it vigorously as if to shake the madness out of it. He tried to evoke gaps in his memory, emotional gaps. Perhaps in those gaps there might have lurked other moments of madness. He could not recall any.

The Devil, in order to deceive men, lets them think he does not exist. And now the Devil was deceiving him.

But no! There had been a valid reason, of course there had been a reason. Of course! *An absurd reason* he could not yet come to terms with.

It lasted for a moment. Then he went back to staring at the television. He saw a church that seemed familiar. A neo-romanic style that was almost pleasing to look at. It must have been the church of Our Lady of Pompeii, in Greenwich Village, the gathering place for Catholic Italians.

The caption spoke of a heinous murder. The cameras were framing the small fountain set up in the garden in front of the building, the small square dedicated to Brother Demo.

Just behind the fountain a priest had been violently attacked. Urgently taken to the hospital, he had died after two hours from trauma and injuries. "I didn't do it," Powell repeated to his inner self, taking his head in his hands once more.

"I didn't do it. I don't remember that. No, there's no way I did it!"

In the meeting room, the detectives were not of the same mind. A palpable belief circulated that it was Powell who had also murdered the prelate.

John Reginald Powell had that cruelty, that *madness* in his DNA. Exactly the same one with which Jacob Madidoff and Phil Grant had been killed.

That ferocity suited the bogeyman, the monster with the axe. Although with the priest Powell had preferred an iron bar.

"What about the little girl? Did he kill her too, then?" Silvio and Mark analyzed the case with Captain Bishop.

"It seems clear as day to me," Bishop confirmed.

"On the little girl's body there are cuts. He could have easily used the axe on her too. In any case, tomorrow we will have the autopsy and the examination of DNA traces found on each of the bodies."

He paused for a moment. Everyone put their thoughts back in order and drew a collective breath.

"All right guys, let's leave the assumptions for now. Silvio, you check Powell's financial situation with Peter Controw, the IT guy. Let's see... Maybe he went crazy because he's burdened with debt." He waved his index finger in the direction of the door inviting Silvio to leave.

"Mark, you go and squeeze that son of a bitch again. Let's see if he finally wants to tell us something about the boys, the priest, and the little girl." The captain closed the discussion.

At that same moment, in his cell, with his ideas and recollections increasingly confused, Powell shivered.

"I have always had respect for priests." He paused to think for a second, letting that sacred figure echo a few times in his mind. The priests... he had always harbored a great regard for the clergy; his mother had taught him that.

Of course, he was in that cell with dull tones and ruined walls for killing. Three, four, maybe five people; he did not know, he had not yet regained full consciousness.

He concentrated and wept. He began weeping when memories rose again, he saw the impulses taking over, flashbacks, shadows, very brief flashes of distorted images. He remembered the two boys perfectly and knew now that they had not been the only ones. He had killed more of them. More than two, certainly.

He believed that when a human being acts according to his primal instincts then he is truly *himself*, he is a *real person,* a self without masks or pretenses.

For a moment he felt proud of this. He had done what needed to be done. Without hypocrisy. This he knew. He felt it inside. But then where did the state of anguish come from?

He returned his gaze to the TV. They were now giving the terrible news Silvio had received at *Wine Temptation*. Behind the low wall bordering the southeast corner of Central Park, bordering Grand Army Plaza had been found the body of a little girl, between eleven and twelve years old. Her clothes were torn, her face was swollen, her legs bruised and bloodied. She still had tears wetting her face and an expression of resigned suffering and surrender to life.

They had beaten and raped her brutally. To prevent her from screaming, they had inflicted so many blows on her that her life had sputtered away amid unspeakable physical and mental suffering.

A uniformed officer in his 40s, tall and slender, approached with a colleague. The coffee machine was not far from Powell's cell.

His hair was barely graying at the sideburns and he wore the uniform of the police force with certain disorder and apparent sloppiness.

He had just returned from Grand Army Plaza. It was he who had caught a glimpse of a small lifeless silhouette thrown into the vegetation. It was he again who had rushed down, breathless with his heart in his throat and especially in the hope of being wrong, feeling the overwhelming desire for his perception to have failed him this time.

Wrapped in a terrifying premonition, he had eagerly hurled himself over the low wall, badly placed one leg, and tumbled down. His body had awkwardly rolled and come to a halt only a few inches from the helpless body of the little girl. Slowly he had risen again, his eyes brimming with horror and his breath choking.

He blanched. His blood had chilled, his stomach had turned over, and he had been forced to move a few feet away to throw up. He had remained, for a few interminable moments, hunched over himself and leaning against a shrub, his legs trembling and his heart racing. He had been in a cold sweat for at least ten minutes.

When he had finally managed to rest his gaze on that innocent being, he had noticed that she was smiling, as if in the last moment of life, she had accepted death as a liberation. The end of suffering, of terror, in the instant when nothing else matters but finding peace.

Liberation from the barbarity of the world.

Calming himself down, he had managed to call the station to activate all procedures: call the detectives, the coroner and an ambulance to transport the body. Exhausted, he had returned to the department and, regaining a glimmer of calm, was now talking to his colleague about how his heart had felt oppressed, suffocated at the sight of wounds on that angel face.

John Reginald Powell listened to everything very carefully, at first with detachment, then slightly more attentively, and he began to think about the two crimes.

The prelate, a poor man, a preacher of good things, sound principles, an example of virtue, and a little girl, a symbol of innocence, with a life yet to be lived, a life cut short before it even bloomed. He felt sorry for both of them, but the phrase that began to resonate in his frustrated and extremely agitated mind was an aphorism by Eisenhower who once said: *after the death of a child nothing is ever the same again and never will be the same again.*

How true!

"Christ, how can this have happened? It is not possible to do this to a child who is only eleven years old," he thought.

That little dress was unfortunately familiar to him. CNN's cameras had framed the little girl's helpless silhouette from above and that single image was enough for John Reginald Powell to recognize the little girl, to distinguish perfectly her colorful dress and especially her face.

He identified it, suddenly, as entirely familiar. The intellect, with its defenses, was still tenaciously trying to erase, to remove the memories, shrouding them in the hazy, opaque fog of the innermost meanderings of the mind.

He could not. The child leapt out of the memories and Powell felt that she belonged in his world.

He tried to tug at his mind, once again, to impose himself to forget. He, the axe serial killer, the ruthless slaughterer, was gripped and completely enveloped by a feeling so dark and oppressive that it cut off his breath.

Suddenly he felt lost. He sensed his soul draining and his heart racing. Then he stood up, his head spinning as if he had drunk half a dozen bottles of whiskey. He placed his hands on the wall and began to give violent blows with his head against the white wall.

"The child, no. Please!" he thought persistently as he hit the wall.

"The little girl, no – the little girl, no – the little girl… NOOOO!" He shouted, finally, with all the breath he had.

Everyone turned sharply toward him. Detective Alessi, who was just heading toward the cell, stopped and stared at him for a few moments.

Powell was still leaning against the wall and was now remembering. Or maybe he wasn't. Perhaps he was just trying with all his might to convince himself that he was in a dream. It could not be true.

"IT CANNOT BE TRUE!" He shouted again and again.

He wanted to convince himself that he was inside a terrible nightmare. Because a *belief* is a fixed idea that takes hold of the mind and permeates it down to the deepest layers, right into the unconscious. It does not matter whether it is true or false.

It is a *belief*. Even if it is not, it becomes TRUE.

That desperate scream, at any rate, could perhaps also reveal that Powell's insipid, somber consciousness was experiencing a rather unexpected jolt. Silvio Brugger ran to Mark Alessi and together they approached the cell.

Slowly.

"There is a glimpse of light even in the darkest of men," Mark said in a low voice. This phrase, uttered two thousand years earlier by the Roman emperor Hadrian, was a favorite of Detective Alessi, who never missed a chance to repeat it whenever the opportunity arose.

He had always been an eternal optimist, and now he glimpsed, in that desperate cry of John Reginald Powell, a chance that the killer would finally repent, that he would decide to confess, fully and comprehensively, to the events of the last few hours. That he would finally empty his conscience and regain a modicum of normalcy.

"Look Powell. I don't know what you're thinking. What I do know, though, is that there are two incredible advantages to confessing," Brugger began in a calm and conciliatory tone.

"The first is that if you confess we will help you by putting in a good word with the prosecutor. The second – well, the second is by far the most important." Silvio paused and let Mark continue.

"Do you have any idea how to live your whole life with such a burden on your conscience? We have experience, trust me. I can guarantee you that releasing yourself and letting out all the bad will make you feel better, much better. A feeling of incredible freedom. The freedom to finally breathe again without the oppressive weight of remorse."

There were moments of silence. Powell did not react. He remained stuck in his thoughts with his head against the wall.

"Tell us about the child if that would help. Then you tell us about the priest and the boys. We can take it one step at a time if you like, you know." The detectives were almost begging the suspect. They were trying to make him understand that clearing his conscience would help everyone, first and foremost himself.

It was one of many interrogation techniques used by the FBI. Probably the most objectionable, as it was highly suggestive, but certainly the most effective.

The tremendous experience gained by detectives told them that when a suspect is on the verge of breaking down you have to be gentle, condescending, and avoid aggressive behavior. You have to take them by the hand, accompany them on a kind of psychological journey that instills serenity, which leads to relief of conscience, liberation and confession. It always works. With the mentally disturbed, at least.

With mobsters a little less so.

John Reginald Powell remained standing. He moved, hunching in pain and despair, to the center of the cell. He moved in small steps forwards and backwards. Tears slid copiously down his cheeks between his unkempt beard and scabs of blood. As they fell, they formed small pink stains on the gray floor.

Sometimes he would cross his knees and draw a circle with his feet. As was always the case, the memories were slowly returning.

He was now remembering the priest, yes. The kind and helpful Italian priest. He had something to do with that priest.

Of course. But what?

He did not know what, but the glimpse of that church on TV had a familiar silhouette. He lifted his arms, arched his back backward, and let out a desperate scream. Then he took his head in his hands again and whispered, "I'm not a monster, Detective…," spitting out droplets of tears that had slipped to his lips.

"The child no, THE CHILD, NOOO! My God, it's just a dream, please. WAKE ME UP, I BEG YOU!"

He lifted a pleading look and met Mark Alessi's eyes. Then he fell to his knees, grabbed the bars of the cell, and burst into desperate weeping.

The axe killer was on the verge of breaking down. Maybe.

CHAPTER 19

Our first and best teacher is our heart.

Proverb of the Cheyenne People

It was the first day of school in New York City. Little John Reginald Powell was at once nervous and excited.

He was visibly thrilled because he could finally leave the dreariness, the musty smell, and the muffled shouting of that dark, claustrophobic apartment. He wanted to get away, to go outside, to walk, to meet people, to talk to someone. Maybe he would even be able to run, spreading his arms wide with his eyes closed, letting the crisp morning air caress his cheeks. Who knows.

He was experiencing it as a prisoner experiences his newfound freedom after years of incarceration. He imagined that he could maybe even play, laugh, joke and do normal things that a child does. Not him.

There were no *Great Tractor Roads* in New York, he knew he would not hear the chirping of the cicadas, he would not be kissed by the blindingly hot sun, but he still remembered the thousands of sparkling lights he had seen upon arriving in the brightest city in the world.

There had to be something, a merry-go-round, a park, an outdoor place where the immense energy contained in that little body, barely four feet tall, could be unleashed. And surely there he would also meet new friends, and new and exciting playmates.

Yes, he was confident.

Yet, at the same time, he was still anxious and lacking certainty. There was a chance that city kids would not share the same passions, that they would likely tease a child who had just arrived from the Deep South. He felt inside, subconsciously perhaps, that he would have a hard time fitting in.

Reginald was extremely well-behaved in school; he was so good that it was difficult for others to understand him. He didn't tell lies even when it was necessary to tell them, he didn't ditch school, he didn't make fun of teachers, he didn't steal snacks from chubby kids, he didn't play marbles outside the door. It was difficult for everyone to figure him out, to the point that some budding little bullies sensed some suffering in him and decided to protect him.

In return, Reginald had to volunteer for classroom readings, pass homework, and help cheat on exam papers.

He harbored a lofty ambition; that of pleasing all the teachers but, above all else, he wanted his father to never be disappointed in his performance and behavior.

His father and also his mother.

Because Reginald knew that she, too, from up there, from the sky beyond the clouds, would scrutinize, judge and appreciate him.

Every time he completed a good deed, displayed praiseworthy behavior or got a good grade, he had a dream.

The little boy dreamed of his mother, whose long, slender hands caressed him as she whispered "good boy" in his ear in a faint voice. His mother had never failed to give her child encouragement, approval and admiration.

In his sweet dreams Reginald could clearly feel the touch of her cheeks on his hair, her light breath as she whispered in his ear, *"You did good today, my son."*

The dreams went on for a while. Truth be told, he never stopped dreaming of her, of being accompanied in the secret meanderings of sleep by a safe, reliable and loving guide. Reginald grew older but his mother did not. In dreams you cannot grow old, people stay the age they were in our memories, no longer young, no longer old. In dreams you don't change, wrinkles don't appear, you don't become cranky, your hair doesn't turn white.

It remains an image as vague as it is welcome.

On Reginald's nights his mother always appeared with a sweet, benevolent and sincere smile. She would hold out her hand to him and whisper tender phrases that in the morning, almost always, little Powell could not remember. Not distinctly.

He knew she would want good grades from her son; John Reginald knew that she would be proud of a polite and respectful child. That was the way to know she would be gratified and proud of her grownup son.

Perhaps his schoolmates had seen in his eyes the emptiness that is left by an absent mother. The sadness of a little boy who could not yet fully feel joy for anything. A person who lacked a light in his soul, lacked a mother to run to, to tell about his first experiences, his first friendships, a new school, a new city.

What was missing was a nice *Great Tractor Road* where he could run, compete, unleash the immense energy that was stored in his legs, whose muscles appeared more defined every day. His friends from down south were not there, and Marion was not there. The colors were missing; the yellow of the sun and corn, the green of the corn leaves, the blue of the clear sky.

John Reginald Powell was in his temporary cell at the department and found himself staring at the white, uneven wall. There were no mirrors in that prison surrounded by high, black bars on two sides, and walls steeped in suffering on the other two.

No mirror this time. Staring at the wall, however, Powell's eyes became alienated, and he imagined that there was one large, crystal clear mirror, capable of reflecting not only the silhouette but also the ethereal colors of the soul.

But he could not see them. In his soul there was only a deep darkness. He gazed for a long time at the human figure his imagination had printed on the wall.

He was not the same man. The child of Baton Rouge had transformed, had grown up.

Could they ever have been the same person, that child running through the fields of Louisiana and the resolute, muscular, mature, blood-soaked man who had committed a massacre the night before?

Would it have been absurd to think that two different people, with two different souls, different physical appearances were united only by a common memory?

No! It was far from absurd.

Reginald knew very well that those two people were the one and the same, the protagonists of a single life, taken only at different times and whose meaning could only be grasped by following, step by step, its entire course.

Life is certainly a continuous transformation. Nothing remains unchanged.

Existence is constantly renewed by a sequence of opposing events, joy and melancholia, pain and pleasure, health and sickness.

The result is a new person every day, different every day, transformed every day. A layering of events that shape, transform and mold us.

But how could it have happened that that mighty middle-aged man, reflected in the false mirror, had turned into a monster?

He felt empty. Like a body falling into the void, plummeting from the roof of a building and no longer in control of itself, with nothing to hold on to, unable to stop. The fall allows no return. One waits for the impact with the ground crushed between terror and reassurance.

His soul had surrendered to madness, without the faculty to stop, dragged to the bottom by the violent nature of that insane and dark fire.

He remembered a great teacher, Seneca.

The best thing, in order not to get caught up in the wrath, is to despise the first symptoms right away, he had read a thousand times in his books. But Powell never could. Recent events would not have allowed the most virtuous of men to reject the ephemeral comfort that wrath brings, even when it leads to madness.

The comfort the thought brought was short-lived. What had happened would never be erased, like a deep and lacerating wound, it would all remain there for eternity.

Branded on the heart.

Reginald lowered his gaze and at that very moment remembered everything perfectly, distinctly. Anger and agony again seized him, gripping his spirit.

Powell lifted his gaze, his nostrils dilated and he clenched his jaw. Then he jerked up on his legs, back straight and taut. He grabbed the bars again. He clutched them and began to tug them with violence and frustration, as if he could somehow uproot them. He forcefully tensed all the muscles in his body as if he wanted to channel all his energy into his hands, in an attempt to break the tempered steel, the paint faded only on the bars against which inmates lean.

In less than a minute he was sweating again, his face covered in droplets that suddenly began to join together on his forehead and slide down to his cheeks. Even his shirt was soon soaked with sweat again, behind his back, on his chest and under his armpits.

His eyes became red again, with blood, hatred and despair. They were filled with an evil fury.

He clenched the bars even tighter with his hands, clenched his teeth and emitted a deafening scream as his entire body trembled and sweated, completely awash in seemingly unreasonable alienation.

The sky had been clear and limpid during that whole terrible, bloody weekend.

It doesn't happen often in New York City. The northern currents carried in clean air and caused temperatures to drop, freed the atmosphere of humidity and briefly cleansed the city of the smog and pollution produced by its nearly ten million inhabitants.

At about 11:30 p.m. on that Friday, what anyone would call an ordinary Friday, something had happened.

The evening was light, clear, as if the bright, large disk of the moon had forced the darkness to stay crouched in a corner, not to intrude on that night, not to envelop with its darkness the buildings, the streets, the parks.

Among the citizens of the Big Apple surely someone had already crawled into their bed, perhaps after a busy day at work. A few lucky ones were making love, a few, probably most of the residents of that fragment of America, were sitting in front of a TV, with a beer in one hand and the remote control in the other. Still others, more mundanely, were shattering what little intelligence remained on social media.

Finally, there were those ready to enjoy the most intoxicating night of their week, the enjoyers, the lovers of life, fun, clubs, cocktails, talk, and friends.

Those for whom life is work but also fun. Those who look forward to the weekend to clear their minds, to have a good time, who depart from Friday night to arrive on Sunday exhausted, happy, tired and fulfilled.

The most privileged were enjoying the view from beautiful stained glass windows elevated to the top floors of one of New York's many skyscrapers, perhaps with a flute of Italian white wine or a glass of fine Scotch whiskey.

The extraordinary diversity of New York's cosmopolitan population makes it one of its most striking attractions.

English, Irish, Italian, Chinese, African American, Native. People of color and whites, with almond-shaped eyes or large black pupils. An extraordinary richness given by the multitude, the conglomeration of languages, cultures, artistic sensibilities and musical tastes.

A massive population, each individual completely different from one another, yet infinitely *similar*.

Well, maybe not entirely similar.

A car at high speed turned onto West Drive in Brooklyn. Inside that car was someone who was driving around the streets of the metropolis with intentions that were anything but noble. Someone for whom the bar of fun, of weekend entertainment, had to be raised at every step.

No, the flute of wine would not have been enough, not even a simple evening with friends in the clubs of the Village. It took more than that to quench his spirit that night.

In the darkness of Prospect Park, the car turned inward and slowed down as it apprached the dog beach. It was deserted at that hour. The car turned off its headlights and slowed down. The tires slid from the asphalt to the breach with a dull clatter. The scratching crackle of the wheels on the dirt road barely managed to break the silence of that place nestled among the trees, made at once charming and gloomy by the ivory-white light of the moon that mixed its pale rays with the yellowish light from the few street lamps scattered here and there.

The car reached the small body of water, a tiny pond where, during daytime, dozens of dogs like to splash around, especially on hot summer days. The light from the car's rear stop lights colored the ground and surrounding trees in a dark red for a moment.

Even for the most depraved beings, those who constantly mock life and death, who trample on dignities, who usurp the freedoms of others, there are limits imposed by conscience. Limits that can be moved forward, and then forward again; but never indefinitely. At some point one must stop, say enough is enough. But sometimes when you say enough you are already beyond the boundary of life.

A door opened. A man got out silently. He held a petite body in his arms.

Small, lightweight. The limit had been moved far over the line. The thin, white arms and slender and bloodstained little legs hung limply and dangled up and down to the rhythm of the man's steps. The head let long hair slide downward, hair that floated free like silk, as if it had been attached to a still-living body. The eyes were half-open and glassy, dulled by terror and the violence of humanity. Eyes that seemed to be searching for the sky. But only in appearance. There was no look in those lifeless eyes.

The man lowered his gaze to stare into her face one last time. He looked at her with a satisfied appearance; she was his trophy. As the moon shone its reflection off the glass pupils between the lifeless child's half-closed eyelids, a faint hilarity took hold of the man.

He smiled. Then, with a twist of his torso he gathered momentum and flung the little girl's body into the water.

There was a dull thud, as if Mother Nature had ordered her creatures to observe in respectful silence. For no one should ever be snatched from life. Indeed, one should tiptoe out of it and only after having realized one's dreams, enjoyed one's joys and experienced its moments of happiness.

The child had not yet matured ambitions, had not lived life enough to draw up her plans. But she had had dreams, that child. Her vivid imagination convinced her that she could one day become a model or perhaps a famous actress. Sometimes she wished she could be a princess in a great castle.

It was a beautiful castle, built out of the stuff of dreams.

But the castle had collapsed, ended up at the bottom of the pond, face down in the muddy bottom as small patches of that little white dress surfaced above the shallow water.

The dream castle collapsed and made no sound because dream castles make no sound when they fall.

The car restarted with some haste, causing the wheels to skid on the breached ground. Parts of the crushed stone, some small fragments, ended up in the water. Sinking slowly, they undulated in the water until they rested gently on the battered, lifeless body of the little girl.

Silence was master once again.

About a kilometer further away, at the Prospect Park exit, a boy was walking with his dog. Days later he would testify that he heard screams coming from a vehicle that came running out of the park's inner road and onto West Drive. Screams of despair or joy, screams of terror or festive exaltation, of wrath, revenge or madness.

He could not say.

The car had vanished. The boy had continued his walk with the dog.

CHAPTER 20

There are two ways to see life. One day closed between two nights, or one night closed between two days.

Yara Gambirasio

The sky had been clear and limpid during that whole terrible, bloody weekend.

It doesn't happen often in New York City. The northern currents carried in clean air and caused temperatures to drop, freed the atmosphere of humidity and briefly cleansed the city of the smog and pollution produced by its nearly ten million inhabitants.

At about 11:30 p.m. on that Friday, what anyone would call an ordinary Friday, something had happened.

The evening was light, clear, as if the bright, large disk of the moon had forced the darkness to stay crouched in a corner, not to intrude on that night, not to envelop with its darkness the buildings, the streets, the parks.

Among the citizens of the Big Apple surely someone had already crawled into their bed, perhaps after a busy day at work. A few lucky ones were making love, a few, probably most of the residents of that fragment of America, were sitting in front of a TV, with a beer in one hand and the remote control in the other. Still others, more mundanely, were shattering what little intelligence remained on social media.

Finally, there were those ready to enjoy the most intoxicating night of their week, the enjoyers, the lovers of life, fun, clubs, cocktails, talk, and friends.

Those for whom life is work but also fun. Those who look forward to the weekend to clear their minds, to have a good time, who depart from Friday night to arrive on Sunday exhausted, happy, tired and fulfilled.

The most privileged were enjoying the view from beautiful stained glass windows elevated to the top floors of one of New York's many skyscrapers, perhaps with a flute of Italian white wine or a glass of fine Scotch whiskey.

The extraordinary diversity of New York's cosmopolitan population makes it one of its most striking attractions.

English, Irish, Italian, Chinese, African American, Native. People of color and whites, with almond-shaped eyes or large black pupils. The multitude, the conglomeration of languages, cultures, artistic sensibilities and musical tastes offering an extraordinary richness. This massive population, each individual so different from one another, yet infinitely *similar*.

Well, maybe not entirely similar.

A car at high speed turned onto West Drive in Brooklyn. Inside that car was someone who was driving around the streets of the metropolis with intentions that were anything but noble. Someone for whom the bar of fun, of weekend entertainment, had to be raised at every step.

No, the flute of wine would not have been enough, not even a simple evening with friends in the clubs of the Village. It took more than that to quench his spirit that night.

In the darkness of Prospect Park, the car turned inward and slowed down as it neared the dog beach. It was deserted at that hour. The car turned off its headlights and slowed down. The tires slid from the asphalt to the beach with a dull skid. The crunch of the wheels on the dirt road barely broke the silence of that place nestled amongst the trees, seeming both pretty and grim in the ivory-white light of the moon, its pale rays blending with the yellowish light from the few street lamps.

The car reached the small body of water, a tiny pond where, in the daytime, dozens of dogs liked to play, especially on hot summer days. For a moment the light from the car's rear lights tinged the ground and surrounding trees dark red

Even for the most depraved, who constantly mock life and death, who crush dignity, who usurp the freedoms of others, there are limits imposed by conscience. Limits that can be moved forward, and then forward again; but never indefinitely. At some point one must stop, say enough is enough. But sometimes when you say enough you are already beyond the boundary of life.

A door opened. A man got out silently. He held a petite body in his arms.

Small, lightweight. The limit had been moved far over the line. The thin, white arms and bloodstained legs hung limply moving to the rhythm of the man's steps. Her hair floated free like silk, as if it had been attached to a still-living body. The eyes were half-open and glassy, dulled by terror and the violence of humanity. Eyes that seemed to be searching for the sky. But only apparently. There was no life in those open eyes.

The man lowered his gaze to stare into her face one last time. He looked at her with a satisfied glance; she was his trophy. As the moon reflected off the glassy pupils between the lifeless child's half-closed eyelids, a faint hilarity took hold of the man.

He smiled. Then, with a twisting movement he gathered momentum and flung the little girl's body into the water.

There was a dull thud, as if Mother Nature had ordered her creatures to observe in respectful silence. For no one should ever be snatched away from life. Indeed, one should tiptoe out of it and only after having realized one's dreams, enjoyed one's joys and experienced its moments of happiness.

The child had not yet developed ambitions, had not lived life enough to draw up her plans. But she had had dreams, that child. Her vivid imagination had convinced her that she could one day become a model or perhaps a famous actress. Sometimes she wished she could be a princess in a great castle.

It was a beautiful castle, built out of the stuff of dreams.

But the castle had collapsed, ended up at the bottom of the pond, face down in the muddy bottom as small patches of that little white dress surfaced above the shallow water. The dream castle collapsed and made no sound because dream castles make no sound when they fall.

The car restarted with some haste, causing the wheels to skid on the breached ground. Some gravel ended up in the water. Sinking slowly, it undulated in the water until it rested gently on the battered, lifeless body of the little girl.

Silence was master once again.

About a kilometer away, at the Prospect Park exit, a boy was walking his dog. Days later he would testify that he had heard screams coming from a vehicle that came rushing out of the park's inner road and onto West Drive. Screams of despair or joy, screams of terror or festive exaltation, of wrath, revenge or madness.

He could not say.

The car had vanished. The boy had continued walking the dog.

CHAPTER 21

A man of war in times of peace fights against himself.

Gaius Julius Caesar

"**I** don't fucking feel like it. Why do I have to write these fucking reports, huh?"

"What's the matter Mark, is it National Blasphemy Day? Get a grip, okay?" Captain Bishop reprimanded Mark Alessi. The Captain was a person of courteous disposition; he didn't like foul language being used at all. Not within the department and, to be honest, not outside either.

But the real reason for those outbursts was much more mundane than one might have thought. Mark did not like office work. He hated it; he hated paperwork. That was all.

Detectives Mark Alessi and Silvio Brugger had gone to the Planetarium Hotel. In room 532, they had found a young man lying on the floor lifeless, apparently in his mid-20s, half-naked, probably just out of the shower. He was wearing only a white towel wrapped around his waist and slippers with the hotel logo still tucked onto his feet.

The boy's face was immersed in a pool of blood. His body was lying disjointedly with his arms down along his sides unnaturally. This position unequivocally meant that the victim had not even attempted to curb his fall.

He had been dead, or at least unconscious, before slumping to the ground.

His hair was black, longer on top and shaded at the nape of his neck. His beard, trimmed with manic precision, was probably cut to show off his facial features: pronounced cheekbones, a square jaw, and thin lips.

At least that was the impression. His left cheek was facing upward, and his right cheek was against the floor.

Mark Alessi had enacted his usual ritual. Leaning with his back to a corner, he had lowered himself to his haunches and carefully scanned the crime scene. A meticulous reading of all the details of the room in order to notice any inconsistencies or objects out of place. The clues!

He observed the room carefully but could not take his gaze off of the boy's eyes; they were open and bulging. The sudden flight of life had allowed the victim no time to close them. They had remained wide open, frightened, horrified. Eyes filled with sudden terror.

There were visible red splashes on the walls as if they had been shot from a fire hydrant; huge, dense drops that had then run copiously down the wall drawing macabre purple rivulets. It was clearly the jet of a violently punctured artery. The sheer amount of blood made the scene look fake, as if it belonged to a movie set.

Staring at the gash on the lifeless body, however, Mark had immediately identified the source of the copious stream of blood spat vehemently on the white wall. A deep, dry axe blow, precisely delivered in the crease where the neck becomes shoulder, at a nearly 90-degree angle exactly in the middle of the cervical spine, five centimeters below the atlas.

The neck had not been completely severed but only just; a few shreds of tissue and perhaps a portion of cervical vertebrae had managed to prevent the head from detaching from the body and rolling on the floor. Apparently. The next day, the autopsy would leave no doubt. The slash had been hurled with such violence that it had passed through tissue like a hot blade cutting through butter. First the neck, then the vertebrae, and finally the carotid aorta, which, once split in two, had erupted so much blood that the body emptied in seconds.

Frank O'Brian, the medical examiner, could not say whether death was instantaneous or had come in slow, excruciating, interminable seconds. Probably the latter. The latter because usually after the rescission of the aorta, for a few moments, the heart carries on beating, fueling the contractions with adrenaline and terror, and increasing the effort with growing fatigue to try to counter the rapid slipping away of life.

The heart muscle did not know that its efforts were ending outside the body, that its furious beats were producing huge spouts and running streams that ended their course first on the walls and then on the floor.

It had gradually emptied out; it had gradually slowed down its beats, slower and slower, until it became silent, stopped.

The killer had not bothered to clean up his tracks. He had left footprints of a number 45 shoe. A shoe whose sole design perfectly matched those of John Reginald Powell.

For Mark, the case could be closed there. He did not drag out his personal ritual. It was not necessary. He rose to his feet and nodded to Silvio.

They already knew who the killer was. They knew they had him in custody, they just had to find the key to get him to talk, to get him to bring up everything: the motive and the exact number of victims; as for the rest... Once the killer is found, the case is closed.

It would be the judge who would see to it that the monster Powell remained in jail until the end of his days.

But justice doesn't work that way. Mark Alessi knew this very well.

"To go to the judge you need evidence. And then you have to bring all the murders together in one procedure, and prove the motive and will of the murderer to prevent a zealous lawyer from trying the path of pleading insanity," his friend and colleague Silvio Brugger repeated ad nauseam.

Of course, of course. On the two detectives' desks now lay several files. A boy murdered in Bryant Park, a little girl killed in Central Park, a priest beaten to death in the vicinity of his church in the heart of Village, another little girl raped and murdered in Prospect Park, and finally a young 25-year-old man found slaughtered in a hotel room in the beating heart of New York City.

What did these victims have in common? Why had Powell chosen them? Most importantly, had poor Phil Grant been the last to deposit his life in the gruesome hands of John Reginald Powell, or would they discover others?

The watchword would be to investigate, *investigate, and investigate again*. Perhaps for weeks, until Powell's wall would come tumbling down.

Or maybe not. Maybe there was a key to access the sick mind of the *Axe Killer*. But if his mind was really sick, the possibility of pleading insanity would have existed in earnest.

John Reginald Powell had regained his consciousness but only partially. He knew that he had killed Jacob Madidoff, the boy from Bryant Park. And he had certainly been the one who had slaughtered Phil Grant, the 25-year-old found in room 532 of the Planetarium Hotel.

The memory was very blurry, the images clouded, but they had told him about an axe, and he had an axe. He deduced, therefore, that it could only have been him.   Then there was the priest, the details of whose murder bounced around in his mind exactly like the scenes seen on TV. Only on TV.

No matter how hard John Reginald Powell tried, he still could not get a clear picture of the priest's murder. He had recognized the square; he was sure he had been there many times. But why he had gone there was still completely unclear to him.

Of the girls he remembered only one. He remembered her very well, to the point of bursting into tears at the slightest resurgence of this memory. Of the other, nothing. Thinking about the girls, however, he inwardly felt such suffering that his brain immediately countered it with real rejection.

His mind wanted to erase those excruciating memories. His chest tightened and he felt that he was suffocating, oppressed by unbearable pain, too much pain even for a sadistic, cynical, and seemingly indifferent killer.

Only three of these victims already had names. Everyone's great worry was that they had not yet been able to identify the girls. Minors do not have documents; parents do not always report their disappearance immediately. Partly because there is a risk of passing as incompetent parents, unable to look after their children. Sometimes it is young teenagers staging brief and not-so-serious disappearances with boyfriends and weekend sweethearts.

"Sift through all existing databases on Planet Earth!" had thundered Captain Bishop.

There was now an absolute need to identify the girls, to understand what could have driven the killer to such a terribly heinous series of murders. Atrocious and different. The image that kept bouncing around in the captain's mind was that of a scythe that had ruthlessly reaped everything in its path.

Powell's killing spree had caused everything else to be put aside. There were no cases to follow except that of John Reginald Powell, the man who inexplicably showed up at Precinct 12 with an axe in his hand, soaked in blood and sweat. Dressed in anguish, anger and madness.

Captain Bishop turned his gaze to the killer, through the glass. He saw him sitting, his head in his hands, seemingly calm. He was motionless.

"The inertia that I call the toil of the spirit." The captain remembered a phrase from Leonardo da Vinci.

Mark Alessi and Silvio Brugger finalized their reports with difficulty. They printed them, signed them, and headed toward Bishop's office. They entered the room without knocking. They had the files for all five murders. They placed them on the desk and took their seats wearily in front of the captain.

No one uttered a single word for three very long minutes. They stared at the folders as if in a kind of trance, each wrapped up in their own thoughts, distracted, almost as if their minds rejected even the possibility of opening those folders and lowering themselves into a grisly and heartbreaking case.

Hell.

A priest, two little girls and two young boys. What united these victims?

"First, are we sure they were all killed by Powell, Captain?", Silvio broke the silence.

"The priest was killed with barbs, the young girls raped, beaten and suffocated, and finally the boys slaughtered with axe blows, dead. Clean blows, hurled to kill without mercy."

"What's the matter with you?"

"I don't think even the cruelest of murderers is capable of as many as five murders in a single day, Captain. There is a lack of time. And then the modalities… they seem like such different *modus operandi*."

"The little girl in Prospect Park has been dead for more than forty hours, Brugger. We're not talking about a single day. Powell had plenty of time to get back to Manhattan and proceed with the other victims. The *modus operandi*, you say? I think that guy has already shown us that he has his own very personal ethics, perverse ethics that are his alone and that we can't penetrate." He paused and resumed.

"Little girls – well, I think he could never have killed two little girls with an axe. What the heck. Not even the worst of monsters, nor the Devil himself would be able to take axe blows to two innocent little girls."

"I say that, at the moment, to speculate is entirely premature," Mark interjected.

"We try to figure out what connection might link the five victims. Let's try and get it out of that madman. We need the motive that drove him to roam the city and slaughter everything in his path. If we succeed, well… everything will be clearer… and if not…"

"I say that for some reason Powell has gone off the rails. Everything that previously represented his world, his city, his life suddenly became his Hell. At that point he decided he would have to wipe the slate *clean*. Kill everyone – but the son of a bitch says nothing. He still seems to be trapped in some kind of murderous rage trance." Silvio broke in softly as he stared at the floor broodingly and only apparently distracted.

Then the detectives took their leave.

At the precise moment the two walked through the door, Captain Bishop's phone rang.

A father and mother had just reported a missing child who bore a striking resemblance to the little girl found in Prospect Park.

CHAPTER 22

God also tried to do things. His prose is man. His poetry is the woman.

Napoleon Bonaparte

Sharon called Mark on the phone. She had managed to carve out an hour's respite from her work and had planned to have lunch with the detective, with her man.

They met at the Food Garage, a very nice place, furnished in good taste. Vintage lamps, industrial-style tables and chairs, warm colors on the walls, wood and green paint. But, above all, friendly staff and good food.

Mark arrived in his usual hurried, eager and hectic mood.

Sharon knew how to calm him down. She had learned in the few months of living together that that whirling, volcanic man had his own switches, his own sensitive spots.

She spoke to him quietly, almost in a whisper. "What's going on, is the new case destroying you?"

"Yeah. That madman... I can't understand him."

"This is nothing new, love. Every case brings you stress..." He smiled, tilting his head slightly on his right shoulder. "That's why the good Lord sent me... to save you." She stared straight into his eyes, letting her smile radiate his face.

These were the strings; this was the main switch. Mark immediately felt drained of tension, relaxed; he drew in a long breath and turned to look out of the glass window. He watched New York traffic flow slowly by. He watched people rushing left and right, some bumping into each other, shoulder to shoulder and pulling straight ahead, without even turning around, without even noticing. Hurried, busy, distracted.

Automata controlled by a system of life that engulfs everything, in which one gets used and sucked in. A continuous and uncontrolled rush, with the sole purpose of working, paying the bills, the mortgage and the car payment. Giving time away, surrendering portions of life.

Everything seemed so normal. It looked like New York City. It was New York City.

He decided that he wanted to enjoy an hour with Sharon as best he could. He wanted to run away with her, of course, if only he could. But he couldn't.

"The system sucks you in," he thought.

There was another case to solve and then there would be another and then another.

Sharon read his thoughts as one reads the pages of an open book. She knew that calming him down was relatively easy for her, but diverting him completely was virtually impossible.

"Did you hear? They found another little girl raped and murdered on Long Island. It looks to be connected with the little girl in Central Park."

"Yes, I heard, of course. That's why I'm so nervous. They're deciding to merge the cases and turn them over – guess what – to the FBI." He returned his gaze to Sharon's angelic face.

She knew; she knew because she had gone to the news. The Washington Post had accommodated her, from Finance to Chronicle. So now they had two complementary jobs, focusing on the same topics; violence, murders, rapes.

They both knew they needed an antidote. They had determined that *work should never be taken home*. The chit-chat about cases, departments, crimes, killers, had to stay out the door.

They almost never succeeded.

They would never be able to admit it, but, deep down, they both knew, albeit unconsciously, how much they could help each other out.

She was an investigative reporter. On many occasions she had been excellent at unearthing interesting if not case-solving details. He, often pretending to talk about it absentmindedly, had turned over details to her that she could publish exclusively.

"Two decent guys, two girls, and a priest. We have to put together five murders, and the only thing we have is a raving lunatic who came to the department voluntarily but says nothing but bullshit on the side."

"What are you trying to tell me, Detective? That I'm going to lose you for some time?" Sharon knew she had embarked on a difficult relationship. On the other hand, her job also had no hours, no rules, few schedules and rare holidays.

A relationship anchored in a very strong, sincere and transparent feeling. Founded on a few simple rules; lots of freedom, lots of trust, and almost unlimited mutual understanding. Their relationship worked because of all this.

"I heard from some side sources about the girls and the priest," Sharon continued. "I know that they still can't say anything but I wish I could do a piece, I don't know – maybe about these crimes in general, taking it broadly. I could write about how violence is on the rise in New York, the usual stuff."

"Yeah," Mark replied laconically, once again turning his gaze outside the glass window.

"When can I write about Powell as well? His story sounds really interesting. I've done some research, you know."

"When you talk like that you scare me. Do you find a massacre interesting?"

"You're right, honey, sorry. The thing is that after a while the human mind gets used to it. It just becomes work. Like pathologists doing autopsies. I would vomit, but for them it's just a lifeless body to open and analyze. My God, how do they do it?"

"It may be true what you say but I can't get used to a massacre," Mark Alessi looked a little blank and disappointed. Coldness did not belong to Sharon, not to the Sharon Flowers he knew, not to the one whom he shared his home with. "... If then there are children... or rather... little girls, raped and murdered...," he looked at the reporter as if begging her, with eyes that were at first red, moist and then finally filled with tears.

"When a child dies nothing is the same, nothing will ever be the same again. President Eisenhower once said that..." Mark had always been a lover of aphorisms.

"You're right, I'm sorry." Sharon lowered her gaze. "The fact is," she resumed, turning back to look at the detective, "the fact is that you barely have time to write about one tragic episode that another one comes to you. You investigate what seems like a heinous crime and then another one comes to you, a hundred times more terrible. After a while your brain goes to mush. Everything goes flat, the wickedness, the madness. It all seems to belong to a plausible, almost normal world."

"It's true. Everything becomes almost normal, for those who don't actually *see* those battered bodies, for those who don't actually talk to the families of the victims, for those who are not overwhelmed by grief. And also for those who don't feel the pressure from superiors who want to solve the case. I mean, sorry but it's all a big mess. Priests, girls... What the hell is going on?" He took a long pause. He took a few sips of his Americano.

Sharon did not interrupt him. She knew when to keep quiet. She read, in Mark's expression, an irresistible desire to vent.

"I feel diseased, Sharon. I think I'm starting to not stand this job anymore." He stared straight into the reporter's eyes. For a moment he thought about how beautiful, joyous and sincere their relationship was.

But it lasted only an instant; his worries returned too quickly. They erased the gentle feelings and catapulted the detective back into reality.

"Too much evil, too much horror. Priests, little girls, young boys. What God could want this?"

"Hey, where has Mark Alessi gone?" Sharon Flowers was determined and knew she had the right weapons. "Where is the fearleass lion, the cop who has solved some of the most devastating cases in this city for the last ten years?"

She bowed his head forward and raised her eyes to meet Mark's gaze, which seemed to be resting listlessly on the coffee cup. She fired her smile again, reached out an arm and grabbed Alessi's hand resting on the restaurant table.

She squeezed it gently.

"I'm here," she whispered to him, "I am here."

Mark winced. That moment of despondency passed like a high speed train, gone in an instant. And it happened because the best medicine for the soul is love. The best cure for the spirit is grace. The best antidote to the poisons of the heart is the sincerity of deep caring. The vaccine against detachment and torpor is the elegance of a kind gesture. A caress.

He stood up, finished his coffee in one gulp, then took Sharon's arm gently and pulled her up a little. She understood and went along with him. He squeezed her tightly.

"I love you," he whispered in her ear, his mouth tucked into her hair.

He walked out of the Food Garage without looking back with a quick, determined step and crossed the street. Sharon followed him with her eyes.

She smiled.

She told herself that this was true love. She had absolute certainty.

"When you love a man's weaknesses, when you allow his life to crowd your life, when you want your soul to permeate his soul, it can only be true love. I love you too, Detective Mark Alessi."

CHAPTER 23

From that day, the sun and
moon can turn as they please,
that I no longer notice
whether it's day or whether it's night and everything in the universe is lost
around me.

J.W. Goethe

He was coming home from school and walked past Timothy Parker's fruit store. He was known by everyone as Old Tim. Old Tim had a beautiful granddaughter, beautiful as the sun, beautiful as a newly blooming orchid with its delicate and naive colors.

Reginald had never been a brash, bold guy and did not dare to speak to her directly for months. He much preferred to approach her respectfully and discreetly, getting slightly closer each day.

In his heart he hoped that she would notice his silent and fleeting presence, his gaze settling lightly on her fast and frenetic yet elegant movements.

He had noticed in her that improper coquetry that arises from shy spontaneity of those who have not yet come to know the pleasures of the world. He admired her cheerful smile, mischievous look, her gentle frenzy, her tall forehead, a symptom of intelligence, and her curls, true charmers of the soul.

He wished she could be his, without possessiveness. She had already seen, in her short life, men use money, power, and influence to gain attention, affection, and sometimes even love. He had seen women take advantage of their sensual and erotic charge to grab men and subjugate them to their love traps.

But what pleasure can a relationship give without absolute abandonment?

Possession is vulgar, it is said. Vulgar and ignorant when aimed at a person.

He wished that Tim's granddaughter, the kind-eyed girl, could be his tender lover, his accomplice, his best friend. An ever-blossoming flower, a graceful face to caress, plump lips to kiss.

He did not know her name. He watched her, studied her, followed her graceful movements in those few seconds when she slowed her pace and passed the side of the counter at the store, or on the street. She sometimes stayed inside, but he could still catch a glimpse of her through a large mirror that Mr. Parker had placed between the ceiling and the wall, probably to check that no one was coming in to steal.

Happiness, by definition, lasts only for an instant, a brief moment. For John Reginald, whose life had been turned upside down and darkened by the events of recent times, by the move to a city where the sun never truly shines... Well, for him, happiness was tucked in those few seconds he could glimpse Old Tim's granddaughter.

He would have liked to take that reflection in the mirror and take it away with him.

Reginald was aware that he was thinking silly things but he did not mind; he knew that in the face of love, human logic is powerless. In his imagination she was Marion, whom he had left behind in Louisiana, whom she resembled very much; Old Tim's granddaughter was only more intriguing, more womanly, more charming, more tantalizing. More grown up.

How beautiful she was. In his eyes she was a goddess capable of bearing dreams and leading his imagination to reassuring places.

She had a high forehead, dark hair and velvet skin. He had never touched her skin, but brushing over it with his eyes was enough to excite his young soul, still insecure and not quite open to life.

He recognized an angelic pureness in her, with an invisible blush and enchanting attitude.

One day it happened that their eyes met. Just for a second.

Her gaze pierced young Reginald's heart like the Crocea Mors, Caesar's sword, pierced its enemies with ease, going straight for the target not to kill, only to upset vital balances and disrupt the paradigms of survival.

What a lethal weapon passed through her long, raven-black lashes. A powerful ray of light shone through her newly found womanhood. Such light was lethal to a young Reginald, who lived almost segregated in a musty apartment building, forced into a life he did not love, that did not belong to him, that did not gratify him in the slightest.

He was waiting for a chance to talk to her, to ask her name, to meet her eyes for more than a couple of seconds.

He had not yet learned the shrewdness of city boys. His gentle spirit had remained that of a simple child from rural Baton Rouge, shy and introverted. Certainly not yet ready to blossom into life, still unaware and awkward.

Life had yet to teach him the contradictions of feelings, the joy that comes with love, the suffering that comes with love, the full and controlled awareness that is always lacking in love.

Love.

He did not know if it was love or if he had become infatuated with that little girl merely because she was a conduit, able to bring his mind and his memories back to Baton Rouge, Louisiana.

She looked like Marion, and he liked to think it was really her. Grown into a woman, moved to New York to look for work. And maybe to try and find Reginald again. Powell could not recognize within his soul whether his was love for Tim's granddaughter or whether, much more trivially, his heart still remained tied to the fragile loves of his Louisiana childhood.

But what did it matter? Passing in front of the store was an event worth the whole day. Like when he waited for little Marion under the big tree, his heart brimming with joy.

And then it happened. It happened, as in the fairy tales, that the girl in the fruit store slipped an apple from her hands and it rolled slowly down the sidewalk until it rested against young Reginald's shoe.

Powell followed with his eyes as the apple slowly rolled toward him and stood petrified. The black-eyed girl stared at him, as if waiting for a courteous gesture. She waited for the little boy to take the apple and hand it to her, to return it graciously.

The girl knew, at that moment.

She sensed in an instant the discomfort, the shyness. She had observed him many times. She'd noticed that as she passed by, that cute, awkward country boy was searching for her with his eyes, trying to scan her movements, to steal her image from the mirror.

Girls know. They know things that boys don't learn until many years later. They are shrewd, intuitive.

Timothy Parker's granddaughter knew why Reginald walked past the store every day; she had noticed him stretch his neck, widen his eyes, smile silently after catching a glimpse of her. She had observed happiness stamped on his round, kind little face with every step.

She also knew his name. On his backpack *John Reginald* was stamped in red letters. A quirk. A way to spend about twenty minutes playing with the marker.

No one would ever take that slightly torn beige backpack away from him. That name was not an ownership plaque or even a distinguishing feature; it had been a game.

But that name, that backpack, that little boy had grabbed the attention of the young fruit seller. She too, through the giant mirror, used to follow Reginald as he walked away. She used to wait for him after school because by now she knew he would pass by.

No one will ever know if that apple fell by accident or if it was actually Tim's granddaughter who skillfully slid the fruit all the way to Powell's shoes. And when John Reginald stood motionless, frozen, she looked at him with the sweetest of looks, the most intoxicating of smiles, and extended her arm, holding her hand out. "Well, what are you waiting for?" She whispered to him, "are you going to stand there all day?"

To John Reginald Powell's ears that voice sounded like a heavenly symphony. The long sought eye contact was now there, meeting his and, through his eyes, snaking its way into his soul.

Reginald bent down without turning his attention away from the girl. He knew where to find the apple. The mind, the heart and the five senses were all perfectly aligned in harmony. He bent down and took the fruit, and felt its smooth exterior. Then he rose again, stretched out his arm and held it out to her.

Tim's granddaughter did not take back the apple. She observed it resting in his trembling palm for a few moments. Then she looked up at him and gently placed her left hand under his forearm, and with her right hand she wrapped Reginald's fingers around the apple.

The contact made the little boy from Louisiana almost vibrate. She sensed everything and with great serenity, keeping her big black eyes on him, she whispered, "My name is Vanessa and I am here every day from two to five to help my grandfather. But you already know that."

She did not take the apple back; she squeezed his hand a little more and pushed back almost imperceptibly, just enough to make it clear that he could hold it.

Not the apple, not just the apple.

Reginald wanted to keep that memory, her smile and lovely silhouette in a corner of his heart. He was not yet fully aware of it, but Vanessa would soon give him a jolt, an emotion he could not have even remotely imagined until that moment.

Surely, he thought as he left, those had been the most intoxicating and intense moments of joy and excitement since he had moved to New York.

CHAPTER 24

When a child dies nothing is the same, nothing will ever be the same again.

D.D. Eisenhower

They entered, eyes brimming with tears. Awareness had crept into their minds, but in their hearts the hope that their little girl was not in those ice-cold rooms was still great.

Mr. and Mrs. Bennett seemed to leap straight out of the previous century. She carried a small, black, faux-leather purse, held composedly by the short handle with both hands joined in front of her and resting on a brown-colored, beige-checkered coat.

Clinton Bennett wore black resin glasses, perhaps more realistically plastic, with thick round lenses. A mousy gray, knee-length coat, with three black buttons buttoned awkwardly over a beer-bellied, sedentary waist that stuck out a few inches. They looked as if they had been catapulted by some bizarre time machine straight from the early 1970s.

He held his hand under his wife's arm, and they both walked with small, timid steps, with the attitude of someone who, without saying a word, is silently begging to not be given that terrible confirmation.

Silvio Brugger had spoken to both parents but made an effort to keep his gaze fixed on the father's face.

Mothers tend to show more of the suffering and heartbreak. Fathers also sink into grief, but they usually react with more composure, letting the anger implode inside a marble shell of disbelief, frustration, and pain.

In contrast, a mother – a mother loses a piece of herself. She is mutilated in body and spirit. A mother loses her breath, and sinks into darkness, into the despair of someone who suddenly has no reason to live.

Silvio would never and for no reason want to take on the burden of communicating to a mother that her sweet and innocent creature no longer belonged to this world. He knew that a mother's pain is unbearable, soul-devouring, heart-destroying. He knew that pain would surely infect him, rest on his soul, heavy as a boulder, and haunt his existence for days, weeks.

Probably months.

Pain that could never reach, however, the unbearable and atrocious level which Mr. and Mrs. Elisabeth and Clinton Bennett were irreparably going to approach.

He had tried to prepare them awkwardly, and yet, the best he could do in such a situation…

"Unfortunately, from the descriptions you have given us, we are almost certain that it is your child. We all hope that it is not, but…," he gently placed his hand on Elizabeth Bennett's arm.

"Madam, be strong." He alternated his gaze on both of them for several interminable moments. "Come, my colleague is waiting," he then said, urging the two to enter.

Inside Mark Alessi was waiting in the company of the legal medic, Frank O'Brian. They saw them approach with deep sorrow already stamped on their faces, with a dark and atrocious foreboding scourging their hearts and souls.

They knew they had to do it.

The Bennetts had enough strength of will and sense of duty to proceed slowly toward the morgue. Yet on the other hand, pressing and harrowing, there was a subconscious scream that cried out to them to flee, to run away from that heinous nightmare.

Mark lifted his arm and rested his hand on Mrs. Bennett's shoulder, inviting her, with a very slight, barely perceptible push, to continue.

Frank O'Brian slid his card over an electronic lock and an opaline-green glass door swung open.

The coroner walked slowly toward a huge steel wall, made up of four rows of refrigerated compartments, closed with shiny, cold doors that looked bleak, sinister, and chilling.

Elisabeth felt her legs give out slightly, her breath shortened and her heart tightened. She had the sensation that she could see all the corpses crammed into the refrigerated cells, smelling of death. At that very moment, she felt her breath break, her soul suffocate.

Something told her that in there, she did not yet know where, lay also her little Alicia. It was her mother's instinct speaking to her, the ancestral, metaphysical connection of a parent with her daughter's soul.

She watched O'Brian head toward a door located below, on the right. She wished she could have stopped time, or at least slowed it down a great deal. She was terrified to find that her worst nightmare was about to turn into reality.

She hinted timidly with her hand as if wanting to block Frank O'Brian from opening that drawer.

O'Brian did not notice. He, too, stood petrified for several seconds, with the handle of the refrigerated door in his hand, already foreshadowing the harrowing scene that was soon to unfold in that room. Then he turned one last time toward Mr. and Mrs. Bennett as if to gain tacit assent; he squeezed the handle a little more and with a decisive snap opened the door.

He pulled outward a sliding metal stretcher on which a tiny body lay.

Detective Mark Alessi involuntarily closed his eyes for a very brief moment. A chill ran down his spine and he prayed that that litter would be, as if by divine intervention, empty.

Clinton Bennett remained motionless in complete apnea, his eyes fixed on the swollen, white face of little Alicia. A face that conveyed suffering and at the same time serenity despite its ashen appearance. She appeared to be asleep, his little girl.

Elizabeth opened her tear-soaked eyes wide, brought her hand to her mouth and held her breath.

Just a few seconds.

Pain gripped her heart with unbearable intensity. She lost consciousness and collapsed to the ground with a dull thud.

Alessi opened his eyes. He bent over Mrs. Bennett to lift her and attempt to revive her. Holding her from behind, arms under her armpits, he pulled her up and placed her helpless body on a chair. Then he begged Frank to get something that could help her regain her senses.

When Elisabeth finally opened her eyes again Mark Alessi realized that a mother's heart would never be able to heal such a wound.

Staring at Elizabeth Bennett's expressionless, tormented face, her body crumpled with sadness and grief in the chair, heartbroken and with glassy eyes, Mark suddenly felt a feeling of rage and hatred tense within him.

He clenched his fists in an involuntary and sudden gesture. He would have liked to summon the murderer there; he would have slit his throat, but only after inflicting unspeakable torture on him. He would have liked to make him feel the same pain that was now gripping that desperate mother.

He recalled when at the department he had feared that Powell's rage and madness might have infected him. He realized that deep-seated hatred inexorably transforms us, unconsciously making us wholly akin to executioners, or animals thirsting for revenge.

With great effort he appeased his anger. He drew a breath.

He swore to himself that he would do everything to ensure that John Reginald Powell was given the maximum sentence.

He was reminded of those moments at the department when Powell had told him about anger, the rage that assaults you and transforms your soul, envelops the will, and scrambles it until it is undone.

Wrath is a brief moment of madness. Wrath wants to lead, it does not want to be led.

He managed to calm himself down. He went back to staring at little Alicia's body, and felt an overwhelming desire to embrace those grief-stricken parents to make them feel the closeness and empathy of a human, before that of the police officer.

He forced himself to resist, and yet still he could not hold back his tears.

Clinton Bennett had meanwhile slumped to his knees and sobbed silently with his hands clasped in prayer. Faith is an anchor of salvation in many cases but there, now, in that freezing morgue, there was no glimpse of salvation for those grief-stricken and laboured souls.

Clinton Bennett watched the medical examiner close the cold room with an immense sense of helplessness and frustration. Then, after a moment of religious recollection, he rose and went to hold his wife with the tenderness of a hurt teenager and the pity that only a grief-stricken father can bring and extend to a mother sunk in despair.

CHAPTER 25

Wrinkles should merely indicate where smiles have been.

Mark Twain

The child from Louisiana had grown up. In the short span of a few years, the little boy from Baton Rouge became a man. He developed a powerful, tall, marble-like physique. Pronounced biceps, defined abdomen and long, muscular legs. The face hollowed out slightly, highlighting black eyes that transferred to the outside world an image of perspicacity, acumen and intelligence while still holding gentleness, nobility of spirit and sensitivity.

He had only partly adapted to life in the big city and, above all, he did not yet have in his eyes the sparkle of madness, of violent and uncontainable alienation, of homicidal rage.

He had become shrewd but never lost his dignified and respectful demeanor. He had certainly retained within himself much of the gentle, transparent and innocent soul of the country child.

Vanessa, already a grown woman, also looked extraordinarily mischievous still. A child who had quickly fit into adulthood, a woman, with soft, thick, curly hair, longlegs, curves pronounced enough to make her extremely attractive. She received constant attention from schoolmates, on social media, and even in old Tim's shop. Yet her heart still beat for Reginald, who in her eyes was still the shy and kind little boy, one who could convey a sense of protection, love, and care with just a glance. An old proverb states *"You cannot fill a cup that is already full."*

Vanessa's heart was already too full of love; there was no room for other flings, other distractions. Over the last months, her love for John Reginald Powell had grown to such an extent that the attentions of dozens of men, more or less young, more or less lusty, more or less interesting, always fell forgotten into the void.

Often, she did not even notice that she was the object of seduction attempts. She gave no weight to the shy approaches, quite similar to those with which Powell had slowly won her heart, and much less to the more brazen attempts. She labeled everything with extreme simplicity, assimilating kind gestures, mischievous pick-up lines, cheeky messages and vulgar groping to simple gestures of friendship, affection and sometimes even gratitude.

Blessed innocence.

Never and under any circumstances did she acknowledge even the most blatant attempts to win her heart or, more low-mindedly, to be able to win her body for a few hours of pleasure.

Vanessa glanced at the street continuously, even when she knew the time was not right. She waited for that prancing silhouette approaching with a frenzied and happy pace, quick and decisive, sometimes even sensual and mischievous.

John Reginald, on his part, could not have wished for anything more.

The ardor with which the mere thought of Vanessa burned and kept his feelings alive was immeasurable. He gave her the most delicate attention, with the most sincere and maniacal care for small things.

It is in the small things that love is measured.

He often spoke to her through body language. He would arrive at the usual time and, as soon as their eyes met, he would hold out his arms and smile. He communicated, with that simple yet blatant gesture, his joy in life, the disruptive happiness he felt simply from seeing her, from having met her.

Then he would stand at the entrance of the store, his elbows resting on the red apple box, his hands holding his face from under his chin, palms and fingers cupping his cheeks.

He flashed a generous grin. A glowing white smile capable of melting a glacier. It made her feel like he was there to admire a priceless work of art. His very own *Mona Lisa.*

Vanessa Parker, Botticelli's Venus. Worthy of admiration, the feminine *Stupor Mundi,* she had the ability to make his young heart beat so loudly it could be heard.

Young Powell gave her all of this. And she responded with a good dose of coyness and mischief. She would turn her back and then twirl her head with the elegance of a princess, and pierce young John Reginald with a glance and a smile, knowing full well that she would make the Baton Rouge boy's eyes swell with admiration and attraction.

Her grandfather witnessed this kind of skit practically every day.

Old Tim would smile. Surely, in his heart, he wished his granddaughter had remained an eternal child, taken as he was by a feeling of jealousy and prejudice of which he was fully aware. But observing the extraordinary spectacle of young love and the happiness printed on Vanessa's face, he could not help but convince himself that it is only right that nature takes its course. Girls start looking at boys. It is only natural.

Mother Nature has her own rules, she wants every human being to have the freedom to discover the foundations of life itself, their own thoughts, desires, needs. It is humans who try to adapt this to their own social, cultural, religious schemes, stifling feelings and emotions in the first place in an attempt to bring everything back into the sphere of asinine "social correctness."

But the intellect suffocates the soul if one attempts to prioritise it. This is because the soul contains within itself both intellect and heart. The soul is feeling, emotion and vibration as well as rationality, logic and judgement.

Timothy Parker promised himself that he would do everything in his power to allow his favorite granddaughter to become the sole architect of her own life, the sole driver of her own spaceship, free of mental cages and social conditioning.

Vanessa Parker would not live a life dictated by others.

CHAPTER 26

They've promised that dreams can come true - but forgot to mention that nightmares are dreams, too.

Oscar Wilde

ark Alessi's phone rang insistently. It was resting on the desk, atop a stack of papers and folders arranged, for once, in almost perfect order. There had never been, and there was no such thing as perfect order in Detective Alessi's work or life.

Mark had always been volcanic, instinctive, sometimes sloppy. But in his chaos he could find anything he needed. Disorder was his natural condition. Utter chaos for others was Alessi's primordial soup; if life appeared as a meaningless jumble of events to others, for him it was the mother's womb, the perfect world, a natural habitat. It was also true for his emotions and moods. He felt appalled by the death of a child, only to rise again with the determination and anger of one who wants justice, and sometimes even revenge.

A whirlwind of sensations, alternating between a meditative and an animated spirit, a docile and gentle soul that knew how to turn into an animal, anxious to be engulfed by passion.

Seeing the bodies of the victims had been too much. Too much even for a seasoned cop, accustomed to the atrocities of a New York City that appeared increasingly poisoned and disturbing to him.

He returned to his desk holding a cup of steaming black coffee. He picked up his phone and noticed the missed call.

He re-dialed the number. It was the coroner.

"Hello Frank, you paged me?"

"Yes, it was to tell you that the autopsy reports have been uploaded into the system. There is also the DNA match on Powell's axe. You can download them if you want. You'll be surprised." Then the phone went silent.

Mark met his colleague Brugger's eyes, who had been watching him curiously.

He knew Frank O'Brian was on the other end of the call, and with a little jerk of his chin, he asked what the news was.

"The reports are in the system. Can you print them out?" He did not have time to finish the sentence. Silvio had already gotten up and was on his way to the meeting room, with giant monitors attached to the walls that could display data, photographs, faces of suspects and statistics. At times it seemed as if trapped in those huge screens was the torture, the ill-treatment, the wickedness of the most heinous crimes. The screens seemed to exude horror even when turned off, those cold and aseptic monitors that had probably never been used to depict a happy event.

Silvio turned them on with a click. After a few seconds, he found the right file.

"John Reginald Powell - victims."

With a double click five more folders opened. They were in alphabetical order:

-   Child 1
-   Child 2
-   Jacob Madidoff
-   Father Antonio Severini
-   Phil Grant

Mark Alessi and Silvio Brugger turned and stared at each other for a few seconds; they knew well what awaited them. Probably two of the worst hours of their lives.

They started with *Child 1*.

Bruised lacerations all over. The child had tried to defend herself as much as she could. Cause of death: *internal bleeding*.

The little girl had in all likelihood been kicked and punched in an attempt to tame her, to submit her to the monster's perverse will, to his cruel urge.

It hardly mattered if it was the innocent soul of a twelve year-old girl. Indeed, considering that there were two little girls so far, the choice of the victims of sexual obsession could not have been random.

The monster had certainly aimed to indulge in the joys of fresh flesh, the excitement of defiling a budding virgin. An object of pleasure, rather than a tender, gentle soul yet to come into real life.

Silvio clicked again and opened a subfolder with photos and other details. Scratches, small wounds, and bruises all over her body.

The report mentioned internal bleeding, a crushed liver, probably from a kick, bruising over much of the body and particularly on the arms and inner thighs

Despite all this, *Child 1*'s face appeared relaxed. It seemed that the little girl had found in the last breath of life a kind of escape. Escape from horror, escape from the devil, escape from a life that had been free and happy until a moment before and then had suddenly become monstrously barbaric.

The detectives had the feeling that in the last moments of life, in the last breath exhaled, *Child 1* had resigned herself to the thought that death would be the only possible relief for her, the only way out. A liberation.

They could not go on. They felt a lump in their throats and breathed hard for a while.

With their cheeks streaked with tears and their souls enveloped in a stupor that left them almost breathless, they both looked away from the screens.

Frank O'Brian, the medical examiner, did not yet know the child's identity when he had created the file on the computer and, sure enough, after Mr. and Mrs. Bennett recognized her, he had forgotten to replace the name. Silvio Brugger clicked on the folder and selected "rename."

He deleted *Child 1* and replaced the caption with *Alicia Bennett*.

CHAPTER 27

I tried to be perfect
But nothing was worth it
I don't believe it makes me real

Sum 41

"Do you know what Seneca, the great Roman philosopher, wrote in one of his letters to Lucilius, Detective?"

His eyes were wide open again, the deranged and mocking smile typical of the psychopathic. His teeth were clenched and his mouth resembled that of a rabid dog. He spat small droplets of saliva onto the table as he spoke.

He waited a few moments, keeping his threatening gaze fixed on the detective as he continued to tilt his neck slowly to each side.

Powell resumed, "He wrote that death has no time and no warning. You should expect it to knock on your door at any time. And I would add... YOU SHOULD EXPECT IT WHEN YOU DESERVE IT, FOR GOD'S SAKE!" He shouted the last sentence vehemently.

"When you deserve it, sure," Detective Brugger echoed him. "But when do you deserve it? WHO DECIDES THAT, POWELL? WHO MAKES THE FINAL RULING?"

Silvio Brugger shouted in turn as he rested both palms on the cold tabletop and thrust his body forward in the direction of the killer.

"You deserve it when you no longer have respect for life itself, when you no longer feel the importance of the gift it represents. Your life and, more importantly, the lives of others," Reginald muttered as he continued to stare Silvio straight in the eye.

His pupils were again dilated with rage, his veins swollen on his neck, and he clenched his fists violently.

Then he continued speaking through gritted teeth, "You deserve it when you no longer know how precious life is. You deserve it when you don't recognize the highest good that God has given us. You deserve it...."

"Yes, yes fine!" Silvio interrupted him.

"You know what, Powell?" Alessi intervened. "You're pissing me off with this bullshit guru talk. Spit out everything you have to tell us or, I swear by all the saints in heaven, that I'll-"

"What, detective? Tell me, what are you going to do to me, huh? Tell me, come on. I am aaaaaaall ears, my beautiful detective."

John Reginald Powell knew how to show contempt. He had no reverential fear, no respect for hierarchy. He lifted his chin and opened his eyes wide with scorn. He knew all too well how annoying the sarcasm was.

He was lucid, cynical, mean. He appeared insane but only occasionally. Other times his unashamed lucidity showed all his crystalline intelligence.

No, he was not a crazy psychopath. Not at all.

Surely the germ of madness must have gripped him for some reason, managing to disconnect, somewhere and for some yet unknown reason, the millions of neurons in his brain. There had been a *blackout* in some recondite part of his intellect. Or, perhaps, directly his soul. Sure, but where? What had caused it?

Wrath, of course.

"Wrath does not want to be led, wrath leads. But wrath is but a brief moment of madness, from which one can turn back."

Mark repeated this over and over again to himself. Powell did not seem to want to turn back at all. On the contrary, he seemed to wallow easily in that sea of anger. No, it could not only be anger that unhinged reason from the common man.

At the FBI, Mark Alessi and Silvio Brugger were fully aware that they did not have many tools at their disposal.

They could and should persuade him to lower his defenses, they should creep into the folds of his madness and try to pull the handbrake. Only that way could they get a full confession, and the case would be closed exhaustively and quickly.

The threats, the shouting, the outbursts, real or fake, alternating with moments of willingness and calm, were merely an expedient, a staging to get Powell on the road to a spontaneous guilty plea.

They were on the right path. So many details were still missing, the number of victims was still not confirmed, and neither was the reason why Powell had decided to attack two little girls, a priest, and two young boys from affluent New York City. Ultimately, he lacked a motive and an interconnection between his targets.

At that same instant, the computer technician, Peter Controw, entered the Captain's room after knocking the door gently twice with his knuckles.

Knocking was just a formality. Controw knew that Captain Bishop, sitting in his black chair, elbows resting on the desk, was waiting for his report.

In it was everything known about the life of John Reginald Powell.

Born in Baton Rouge, Louisiana, moved to New York with his father Joseph, he had then lived an all-too-ordinary life. Schools, college, graduating with high honors from the Institute of Fine Arts at NYU, working with the history and literature department.

He was a professor, a lecturer, an educated man, but above all, one who had built himself up through sacrifice. Described as a brilliant mind, appreciated in academia and loved by his students. He was called as a speaker at numerous conferences, meetings, even a guest on TV shows. An expert in his fields: literature, art, and art history.

He had married, at a good age, one Vanessa Parker with whom he had a little girl, Jamilia. The marriage had then fallen apart, as it happens with so many couples in our time, but the divorce was not described in the report as an adversarial separation. The two had known each other as teenagers, and over time love had faded to first affection, and then respect.

Things had been settled via dialogue, with the gracefulness of reasonable mediation on both sides. Powell's relationship with his daughter was described as normal while a cordial and cooperative parenting relationship had been established with the child's mother.

He had never failed to pay his part, not even for a single month, and was constantly making sure that both mother and daughter did not lack for anything.

Ultimately, he was what is commonly called a good family man, a man of culture, serene and mild in all matters of private and public life.

He had stayed in the Village, not too far from the University campus and his office. From what appeared in that detailed report his true and only interest was just that: art and history.

Between the dozens of papers was a list of various publications, among which were a couple of books on the history of the Ancient Greeks and the Roman Empire that quickly became landmarks for lovers of the genre.

Captain Bishop lifted his gaze in the direction of the interrogation room. He remained motionless and deep in thought for at least a couple of minutes. He stared at the door, his mind absent and confused.

There was no explanation in that report, no trace of the murderous madness, not even a crumb of a clue that could lead one to understand why an ordinary citizen, a well-liked professor, a man worthy of everyone's esteem and affection, could have given birth to an afternoon and night of such absurd violence.

At that moment the Captain wished he could afford not to care. The killer was providing nothing but fragmentary and disorganized information. By now, the media had learned of the five victims, and all over the newspapers, news programs and talk shows there was nothing but talk of a *monster* raging in the city. No one yet knew the details of Powell's arrest, and the pressure was mounting to unbearable levels.

"The Monster," Bishop thought.

Of course, when he thought back to the bloodied man, drenched in sweat, dirty and smelly, his eyes lined red, his temples throbbing, his neck veins swollen and his nostrils flared with rage... Well, thinking back to that man, he would have labeled him as *the Monster,* too.

But reading and re-reading the report, thinking back to the moments of calm, albeit sparse and short-lived, in which John Reginald Powell had been cooperative... None of those thoughts would ever conjure up the image of a blood-thirsty murderer, a madman, a psychopath.

He took his head in his hands and began massaging his temples.

"Knock, knock," he heard a female voice at the door. "May I come in? How are you, Captain?"

"Sharon, come on in."

Simon Bishop got up from his chair with listless, tired movements and walked over to the Washington Post reporter. He stretched out his arm and shook her hand.

"Have a seat," he pointed to the nearest chair. "Yes, thank you. I'm fine." He stalled for a few seconds. Then he resumed. "Of course, we've had better times, although I no longer remember when that was." He smiled sincerely at her. "But I think you're here for Mark, right?"

"Yes. Pardon me, I was just passing by and thought I'd surprise him."

"And he would have liked that, I'm sure. Unfortunately he's still in the interrogation room with that Powell guy that I imagine you know about."

"Yes, Mark has shared something but not very much. He says it's all still privacy protected."

"That's right, although I don't know who benefits from all this secrecy anymore. It is only raising tension in public opinion. If they knew that the killer was caught, probably everyone would calm down a lot."

"Did he not turn himself in?"

"Yes, sorry. You're right. He came on his own two feet... and... with his axe, merciful God, after killing five poor innocents."

"Four, captain. I think there are four victims at the moment. Information has reached the newsroom; it appears that the murderer of Father Antonio Severini has been arrested. A white man in his thirties. He was pulled over for drunk driving and a bloody bar was found in the hood of his car. As well as about five thousand dollars in cash in a black bag. Our sources say it was a drug addict who allegedly attacked the prelate to steal offering money. Every weekend Father Severini would go and pour out the collected sums, nearly five thousand found in the 30 year-old's car, to be exact. I think he is locked up in the 27th precinct right now."

"Well, I see we are always the last to know things," Captain Bishop said lowering his eyes, almost ashamed. "On the other hand, that murder was a little out of context compared to the others. But it was still our case, and I think we'll be given official notice shortly from the 27th," he added to justify himself.

"Of course, I'm sure of that. And I believe that Mark should get the news through official channels. So... Captain..." she rested her hands on the armrests and pushed herself up. "You have work to do and I'll – I'll be off."

She smiled, stood up and waved goodbye with her usual elegance.

The Captain watched her leave, not without a touch of envy toward Detective Alessi.

"Sharon Flowers deserves everything," he thought. "She is no doubt a beautiful woman, intelligent and professional."

He went back to staring at the door of the interrogation room. He leaned his back against the chair and settled his head on the top of the backrest, shifting his gaze to the ceiling.

He squinted his eyes and imagined a tropical beach. The breeze caressed his face, the sun infused him with warmth.

He would choose such a place as soon as he retired. He would run away from New York City, without any doubt.

CHAPTER 28

Years of love have been forgot,
in the hatred of a minute

Edgar Allan Poe

He closed his eyes. For a moment he managed to turn off the voices and screams that crowded in and out of him. He removed himself from the present by going to take refuge in a corner of the universe untrampled by human beings, in a black hole capable of swallowing moods, torment and despair; a kind of mental alienation, a precious refuge made of calm and silence.

He no longer felt like seeing and hearing anyone. He felt pressured, disturbed.

He closed his eyes, relaxed his shoulders by dropping them a few inches and resting his elbows on his thighs. His wrists remained suspended, hooked to the table by means of those annoyingly short chains that held him to the steel bar with almost total immobility.

He recalled in his mind, with all his might, pleasant memories. He must have read somewhere that recalling good memories triggers a virtuous cycle capable of surpassing moments of depression or low mood.

He tried to find, in the meanders of his memory, one of the many joyous occasions, moments of fun and hilarity as well as moments of love and passion. He needed serotonin and endorphins, and could only access them through his memory.

A respite was needed, a *time-out*; the brain was showing conspicuous signs of failing, headaches and nausea. The bombardment of questions, inferences, pictures of dead bodies, screaming, doors slamming, cops coming in and out; all this had to stop.

He took his head in his hands, trying to plug his ears. He shook his head, squeezed his eyelids so hard he began to tear up. His face, hidden in the palms of his hands, was flushed.

Then he drew himself up, let out a hoarse, inhuman scream as if emitted by a gorilla, a dinosaur, an alien being, a creature from a distant planet. The room rumbled and vibrated as if struck by a deadly shock wave.

Powell rose from the seat with a jerk, flung the chair against the wall with the back of his knees and pulled the chains violently until the heavy table was lifted several inches off the ground. His neck showed all its pulsing veins; his eyes looked as if they were on the verge of spurting blood, like in a horror movie; the muscles in his arms were contracted almost to the point of spasm, stiff and hardened by the weight of the massive steel table; his teeth clenched visibly under contracted lips and nostrils flared with fury and hatred.

It lasted only a few seconds.

Then, as had often happened in the last few hours, Powell abruptly regained his composure and returned to his seat. But the chair was not there; it still lay on the floor near the wall. Detective Alessi watched impassively as John Reginald's face returned to a normal color and relaxed sightly. His face was still lined with tears, but his anger seemed to have rapidly died down once again.

Powell thanked the detective who had repositioned the chair in its place. He sat down and rested his forehead on the table, encircling his head in his arms.

He could finally recall his memories, now that silence ruled the room.

He saw the movie of his wedding pass him by. It was a summer day and a light breeze brushed faces and lifted skirts just enough to make all the girls beautiful and mischievous.

It brought with it lightness and joy. The Good Lord had sent him that gentle wind to blow and carry away all thoughts and worries and deliver to him, on those church steps, the best day of his life; of their lives.

Vanessa was radiant, more beautiful than the sun that illuminated her face and left the sun looking dull in comparison to her brightness. She was as enchanting as the clear summer sky; her smile told a wonderful tale, and in her eyes shone a brilliant and sincere light.

She wore a little white dress that hugged her petite and well-proportioned physique, a small bouquet of flowers as befits any newlywed, and an amount of happiness in her heart that no instrument in the world would ever be able to measure.

The church service had been accompanied by a gospel choir but for some inexplicable reason a song by the Goo Goo Dolls resurfaced in John Reginald's mind.

"The title... the title... the title," he thought.

No. He could not remember the title, but it seemed precious, absolutely necessary, like a rock to be clung onto in order not to drown, to save a life.

He struggled as he tried to remember the name of that song. It was important. Not remembering it gave him a feeling of apnoea, made him feel like water was rising to his throat and taking his breath away at times, just like the waves of the sea. The drowning man fights not to drown, he is submerged momentarily, his breath is cut off and there's no air in his lungs, until he finally resurfaces, gasping the breath with all the strength he has. "Yes, there it is." It suddenly surfaced in his memory, just as a cliff emerges from the billows of the sea at the moment when you least expect it, within your reach. A salvation.

"It was *Come to me...*, yes, *Come to me*. I'm sure of it," he reassured himself.

He let out a sigh of relief. He felt reassured and safe. That song had accompanied Reginald and Vanessa for a few years. It was what they would call "our song."

It was definitely the first song they played to little Jamilia. Their baby girl had come into the world after a few years together. Happy years, in which husband and wife had each consolidated their work, Reginald as a university professor and Vanessa by taking over her grandfather's fruit shop and turning it into a store stocking the highest quality food products.

He remembered, now, the first moment with Jamilia.

Reginald had held her in his arms soon after birth, and she had unexpectedly opened her big, black eyes. She had given the first smile of her life and grabbed Daddy's index finger. She had squeezed it with all the strength she had. The strength of a newborn.

Her tiny hand could not even encircle the finger in its entirety, tiny as it was.

Sitting once again in the interrogation room, John Reginald Powell was now again feeling that faint grip on his index finger. He could feel it distinctly.

With his eyes closed, he lifted his finger, as if he wanted to go along with the newborn's gesture, slowly leaned his head over his left shoulder, exhaled slightly and arched the ends of his mouth, a benevolent smile, as if his little daughter had still been there in his arms. He could see her. With his eyes closed he indulged, brought his arms forward and crossed them, in a gesture that imitated a father holding his daughter.

Immediately afterwards he opened his eyes slightly and saw only his hands, massive and mighty, which appeared hollow and bloodstained, dark, irretrievably contaminated with terror, having become a terrifying instrument of death.

CHAPTER 29

And we will not be tomorrow what we were or what we are.

Ovid

"You guys are good. You're probably the best detectives we have. But you're also really good at pissing me off, dammit!" Captain Bishop began the sentence with apparent calm and ended it with a raised voice as he waved a beige-colored clipboard in the air, the kind used by the department.

"What did we do this time?" Silvio Brugger asked, hinting at a slight smile and turning to his colleague Alessi.

"Frank O'Brian told you that all the material has been entered into the database, right? The photos, the autopsy reports, and the result of the DNA analysis on Powell's axe," the captain continued, annoyed by the light-hearted attitude of his coworkers.

"Yes, of course," replied Brugger once again. This time, however, he kept a more serious expression as he invited his superior to carry on.

"Did you at least take a look at it?" asked Bishop.

"Yes, of course. A quick overview... Come on Captain, what's the point of seeing the autopsy results? We already know how they died...," Mark interjected. Then he lowered his gaze and turned to his colleague sitting opposite him. In a more feeble tone, almost in a whisper, he added "Actually... We closed immediately after viewing the first file. Seeing the photos of Alicia Bennet... In all honesty... made us sick to our stomachs." He attempted to defend their actions, behavior that to most would have appeared entirely natural.

Anyone, in fact, would have been distraught before that horror. But the truth is that a detective cannot; a detective must absorb and move on. It's part of his job; he should be trained.

"He MUST be trained!"

From time to time Mark Alessi would pause to reflect on paradigms of this kind, and he often found them difficult to comprehend, to fully metabolize.

"How far have we strayed from God," he wondered, "if we need to train men to endure human atrocities?"

But it lasted only an instant. Immediately afterwards the work absorbed him, permeated him, engulfed him. It was the same for his colleague and friend Silvio Brugger.

"However, we only took a break. A coffee to settle the stomach and soul, Captain. It's Monday morning, Powell showed up Saturday morning, the murders happened on Friday. Come on, Captain... We were here on Sunday, too..." Mark Alessi spread his arms wide and pulled his torso slightly backward.

"What more does he want from us?" He thought, but didn't say.

Simon Bishop caught on quickly. It was true, he couldn't have asked for more. Not from the detectives, not from the medical examiner, not from the officers on duty. They had all been hard at work, with dedication and spirit.

He did not add anything else. He stared at the two of them, then raised a hand holding an envelope.

"Four different DNAs were identified on the axe." He dropped the beige folder heavily onto Detective Brugger's desk and exhaled heavily.

"One is certainly Powell's, he was injured during the various scuffles and he lost blood, we know, he still bleeds from time to time, the bastard.

The second DNA corresponds to Jacob Madidoff and the third one to – what was the name of the third one?"

"Grant, Phil Grant," Silvio promptly retorted.

"Yes, him, indeed..." He paused. "The fourth one does not correspond to either of the girls or the prelate. About the prelate. His killer has been arrested. It seems to be confirmed. It is no longer our business." He drew his breath and resumed, "So there is still one victim missing; the people killed with the axe are three, now we know for sure. As for the girls – we seriously hope that their number remains *two*."

The captain pointed to the still unopened folder on the desk. He squinted, lowered his head slightly, and stood still; his arm outstretched with his index finger swinging up and down, facing that pain-filled envelope.

It was as if in that instant he was intimately reciting a prayer. He didn't know it but the deepest, most intimate part of his heart was really unconsciously reciting a prayer.

"Get to work," he suddenly resumed. "Go to that son of a bitch in there and make him tell you where we find the fourth body."

"No need, Captain." Mark Alessi uttered those three words under baited breath. He stared at his iPhone wide-eyed, with disbelief stamped on his face. A friend, a colleague from District 19, had just sent him a message. Their presence was requested at a garage not far from Bryant Park on 6th Avenue. There a young man apparently in his mid-twenties had just been found, seated inside a midnight-blue Maserati, with an interior that must have been white but was now covered in blood. Blood in which John Reginald Powell was still covered.

Blood on the dashboard, blood on the windshield, on the mat, and blood everywhere.

CCTV cameras had caught everything. When Mark Alessi and Silvio Brugger arrived, they found the janitor sitting in his post looking distraught and with his head down. He was a man in his fifties, pudgy to the point that his uniform looked as if the buttons would pop off at any moment. He had sparse, sticky hair, and, probably because of his conspicuous weight, he also sweated simply by standing still.

At the sight of the FBI he left his post.

"On Saturdays and Sundays, the parking lot is practically deserted," he told Silvio, spreading his arms wide and lifting his shoulders slightly. "People who work nearby leave their cars here, Detective. And on weekends no one works. So... There are very few cars. Who checks them? Who checks the CCTV recordings?" he continued to lift his heavy shoulders and show his palms.

"No one, Detective," he continued. "No one ever looks at them. We always think about it on Mondays. We do the rounds," he made a twirling gesture with his raised arm as if to draw a circle in the air, "check that everything is okay and go back to our post. Only if we notice something unusual, something strange, only then do we check closely and maybe look at the surveillance."

He looked away from Brugger and took a sweeping glance of the parking lot. He was confused, resumed sweating profusely, kept rubbing his greasy hands mechanically, distractedly. He was restless, nervous. He would have gladly burst into tears but managed to hold back with deep breaths.

"That's what we were taught, Detective, but honestly, nothing has ever happened to me in the 15 years I've been here. Everything has always gone smoothly. After all, it's a garage, for God's sake, what could possibly happen in a stupid, insignificant parking lot on Sixth Avenue in the middle of downtown Manhattan?"

"Okay, okay." Silvio interrupted him, "calm down now. So what happened, what did you see this morning?"

"I arrived very early, I start at six. There was the blue Maserati, there on the ground floor, row number 2. I caught a glimpse of it coming down the elevator. I know that car, it belongs to Jack Hecker's son. His name is Martin."

His eyes glazed over, he explained that he knew Jack Hacker very well, the chief financial officer of one of the most active insurance groups on the East Coast of the United States of America. A guy who was always nice, never arrogant and above all very generous in his tipping.

With his son Martin, he was less familiar; he was the scion of a wealthy family, an energetic, exuberant young man, enthusiastic about squeezing every moment out of life and enjoying it to the fullest, all the way.

"I was a bit surprised, detective. The Heckers never leave their car here on a Sunday night. I didn't really want to go and check, it seemed indiscreet. I went my usual route, just a little wider beyond the column."

He pointed to the row of pillars in the center of the garage. His chest heaved as if he were about to burst into tears. He brought his hand to his mouth and whispered between his fingers, "I noticed that there was someone in the car. But with the low light and the glare from the neon lights you could make out a slightly bent head." He interrupted his story and brought both hands to his face to hide a wince.

He apologized. Then he resumed, sobbing, "I didn't go right away to check, I thought he got drunk the night before and fell asleep in the car, from a distance I didn't notice all that blood, my God... I didn't even notice the broken glass on the ground. I was far away..."

Silvio acted distracted. He looked toward the interior of the garage so as not to let the weight of his eyes be felt, feigning almost disinterest in that oh-so-emotional response from the security guard.

Mark, meanwhile, had gone inside to view the footage. The images were sharp, if inexplicably black and white, early 1980s style.

One could perfectly distinguish the boy proceeding with a seraphic, relaxed, slightly swaying gait, probably drunk. Mark watched him search for his car keys in the pockets of his dark overcoat.

Soon after, a second figure appeared, tall, powerful. A black man wearing a white T-shirt on which dark spots of blood were already clearly visible.

He kept his right arm straight down, clinging to his side. In the dimness of the garage, a glint made the screen of the surveillance monitor light up. It was the blade of an axe.

The man in the white T-shirt kept it close to his body, at thigh level, slightly shifted back, to hide it as much as possible from the boy's view if he turned around.

Then the attacker began to lift it slowly. As he got closer to his target, with a quiet pace, his arm stretched upward and he wielded the terrible weapon. The boy, meanwhile, had opened the car door and was about to take a seat in the passenger compartment. Powell was now behind him, only a meter away. At that very instant Martin Hecker had become aware of the shadowy presence and turned his head. Just in time to see the scythe of the *Lady of Darkness* cleave through the air with a dull hiss and thrust into his body.

Mark Alessi saw the boy's terrified look, saw the axe come down hard and land in his chest. He recognized John Reginald Powell.

The Monster.

Powell had been extremely quick. He attacked with one hand, with the other he had then grabbed his victim by the coat at shoulder level and held him up. Then he opened the car door wide with his foot. With a sweeping gesture he turned the boy's body over and threw him on the seat. He watched him contentedly for a couple of seconds. Then, with a violent jerk he had wrenched his axe away from the boy's chest.

At that precise instant, like a bottle of champagne that burst after being shaken and uncorked, the 26 year-old's heart erupted. Blood splashed against the Maserati's windshield and from there, split into a thousand drops on the dashboard, on the steering wheel and everywhere else.

A second regurgitation of blood had followed while Powell, motionless, leaning against the open door, suddenly enjoyed the horrifying and terrible spectacle.

Detective Alessi continued to stare at the screen as if hypnotized. A murder so vicious and so fully documented had never happened to him. He continued to watch the victim at first tremble, then tense every muscle in his body in unimaginable spasms, and finally give up, abandoning life.

The boy's left arm slowly slid down his own body and remained dangling, outside the car.

John Reginald Powell had watched the scene in its entirety without moving a single finger, a spectator; he was visibly enjoying his action. Then, without letting a single ounce of emotion show, he grabbed his wrist and repositioned the arm on Martin Hecker's legs.

He closed the car door and stayed for a few more moments admiring his feat. He had looked around, moved the axe from his right hand to his left, and finally walked toward the exit with a weary but determined step.

After a few steps, however, he returned with great strides, almost running. He grabbed the handle of the axe with both hands and violently struck the glass window on the driver's side.

He then flung his body through it.

The video now showed pieces of glass sticking into Powell's arms.

Without apparently feeling any pain, John Reginald, furious, had relentlessly continued to push himself inside. Despite some pieces of glass tearing his arms and body apart, he grabbed the now lifeless boy by the shoulders and yanked him, back and forth, while from his open mouth he let out a piercing scream, a sound that had reached the surveillance cameras muffled but equally terrifying, full of anger and pain.

When, after several interminable seconds, Powell reemerged from inside the car, his eyes were visibly glazed over and his cheeks clearly streaked with silvery tears. The overlay clock read 5:36 a.m. in the morning. Before long, John Reginald Powell would walk through the door of the 12th Precinct.

CHAPTER 30

Fools rush in where angels fear to tread.

Alexander Pope

"Gentlemen, meet John Reginald Powell."

Computer technician Peter Controw turned on the monitor in the meeting room with his remote control and let Powell's big face appear on the screen. The picture showed a mild-mannered man with gentle features and a slight smile that seemed completely natural and spontaneous.

He had not posed for the photo. That smile was one with his face , naturally embedded in his features, as in Leonardo da Vinci's *Mona Lisa*. Detectives Mark Alessi and Silvio Brugger had a moment of hesitation. The man held in the department's cell had rage stamped on a face tense and hardened by hate. The murderous fury had transformed his features, destroyed the kindness of that face and killed his smile. It took them a while to realize that the man on the monitor and the man locked in the department cell were the same person.

"Lecturer in history and philosophy at NYU. Originally from Baton Rouge, Louisiana, he moved to New York forty years ago. He lived with his father Joseph in an old apartment building in Queens before winning a scholarship to NYU, in fact. He married Vanessa Parker but the two divorced three years ago. They have a little girl who now lives with her mother. He is described as quite approachable with students, his relationships with colleagues are friendly and, apart from an inactive social life, he does not appear to be a sociopath at all, far from it. Turns out he subscribes to philosophical journals, theater seasons, has been registered as a guest speaker at several conferences, has a subscription to Netflix, Amazon Prime, Spotify... a normal person, in short."

"Tell us about his childhood. Why did he relocate from Baton Rouge to New York?" intervened Detective Brugger.

"I see what you're getting at, Silvio. Serial killers often become serial killers because as children they suffered violence and mistreatment. But in this case we have no record of that. His father was mild, old-fashioned, a gentleman as some would say. They moved to New York after his mother died of bone cancer. Probably the father simply wanted to make John Reginald forget the tragedy as quickly as possible. It may be that he decided to distance him from anything that might remind him of his mother."

"I understand," Brugger added reflectively. "Being uprooted from the places of childhood as a result of such a serious and profound bereavement can be traumatic for a child, but I don't think that could have triggered, forty years later, a murderous rage, do you?"

"Such serious and profound grief..."

Silvio's words rumbled through the room and unexpectedly settled heavily on Mark Alessi's thoughts.

The detective became estranged and began to think about what weight a single event might have.

"Losing your mother," he thought, "must be the greatest tragedy a child can experience. Because at ten, eleven, twelve, you are no longer a child and you are not yet an adult. You are in that middle ground where the trasformations of body and soul demand support and care. Not physical but metaphysical. A presence, a closeness that instills a sense of security and serenity. A presence that can only be given by parents, the only ones who are able to relentlessly give their love, always and unconditionally. Losing a mother at that stage could result in a storm that overwhelms, an emptiness that oppresses, the unconditional and pure love that is mercilessly mowed down by adverse fate. It could break the thin thread that keeps your mind clinging to the prospect of a peaceful life. A young boy could easily be shocked, begin to resent the whole world, hold it responsible for that misfortune. An anger that remains latent, that keeps at bay somehow, until it explodes, for some obscure reason."

"Do we know where he lives? We need to go take a look at his house," Silvio asked without taking his eyes off the giant screen that lit up the room, interrupting Mark's stream of thoughts with his deep voice.

"Yes, of course. After the divorce he moved to a small apartment in the Village, on Groove street. You'd better talk to the captain. I don't think it would be difficult to get a search warrant." He spoke the last sentence with an ill-concealed and perhaps unintentional ironic tone. After a moment of reflection he added a couple of remarks.

"See if he left his cell phone there. When he arrived here he didn't have it with him. It seems to be turned off and I can't track it down but I think taking a look at it could give us useful information. A professor certainly also has a computer, a laptop, maybe a tablet. In short, take what you find. If we're lucky we might find pictures of the victims and figure out if he had been following them for a long time or if he really picked them randomly."

Silvio and Mark remained silent, each absorbed in his own thoughts. Each imagining the home of a history professor, of an art enthusiast.

Of a serial killer.

CHAPTER 31

O Great Spirit,

Give me the strength to endure what I cannot change
And to change what I cannot bear.

Prayer of the Comanche tribe

He had completed his massacre. Leaving the parking lot, John Reginald Powell had found a flower bed bordered by a small wall. He sat down to rest.

After drawing his breath, he decided to wait for dawn before walking toward the precinct. Yes, he wanted to wait until dawn, and as he turned his gaze to the east, he realized that it would only take a few minutes; the glow of dawn was already recognizable on the horizon.

It was a quiet Saturday morning, with a slight cool breeze coming off the ocean to make that end of spring that already smelled like summer less sultry. New York was usually quiet at that hour, like an elegant lady still sleeping, giving her weary body a respite and relaxing in soft, fragrant sheets of fine silk.

Powell waited for no real reason; to rest, perhaps, or to let the anger blow over, to try to come to his senses. He did not succeed one bit.

He looked for a long time at his hands, which were stained with blood; then, with a sequence of gestures that seemed like something sacred, he closed his eyes, raised his head and drew a deep breath. In reopening his eyes he joined his hands and turned to the sky. No one will ever know whether he wanted to thank God for giving him all the strength and courage he needed or whether he was just invoking forgiveness to the Almighty.

That set of gestures had no less strengthened his conviction that the end had come. The next step would be to turn himself in to law enforcement and serve his sentence, atone for his guilt.

But what punishment could he have possibly served that was more severe than the one he already carried inside him? He stood for a long time observing the sky. He realized that there were no stars, not that night. At first there was black darkness. Then dawn had colored red a thin veil of clouds that would dissolve when the first warm rays of the sun arrived.

As he silently continued to witness the celestial vault, a passage from Dante Alighieri's *Divine Comedy*, the literary work of art par excellence in his personal judgment, sprung to memory.

The memory of Dante who, accompanied by his teacher Virgil, crosses the gate of Hell and discovers that the sky is black. No planets or stars shine in that dark vault saturated with suffering.

Souls in that inauspicious place are ethereal, intangible. Souls made of immaterial spirit yet endowed with a barely substantial and scarcely dense body. Insubstantial and intangible souls in light bodies, tangible enough for them to feel pain, to suffer, to feel the torment of divine retribution. Hell.

That must have been what Hell was, *his* Hell.

Like the supreme poet in the *Comedy*, he too had descended to the depths of the underworld and met his demon, his Lucifer.

But in his work, Dante Alighieri had succeeded in progressing the tale. He tells of an ascent through Purgatory and all the way up to Paradise.

There would be no Heaven for John Reginald. There would be no Purgatory either.

To Hell he had descended and in Hell he would remain to rot, for that was his destiny. In reality it was Hell that had descended into his soul and filled it with hatred; it had devoured it, torn it away without appeal.

But you can only snatch something away from those who resist it. And he had not resisted. Not to hatred, not to anger, not to torment. The Furies, the three Ladies of Cruelty and Vengeance had taken possession of his body and spirit without his realizing it. He had witnessed it as an actor watching a movie in which he plays the role of the protagonist.

No redemption would be there for John Reginald Powell.

And as if all this wasn't already colossal, he was also realizing that spewing all his frustration, unloading his hatred on his victims, giving free rein to his anger by committing a massacre had not served any purpose.

It had soothed the terrible and unbearable pain under whose cloak his soul lay only for a few precious moments.

He had felt relieved with each victim, but that ephemeral feeling unable to satisfy his spirit had only increased his disgust and set Reginald off, like a bloodhound, in search of the next one.

No matter how determined he had been, Powell had not been able to scratch even a small fragment of that inexhaustible and overwhelming feeling of suffocation.

It had remained there, crushing the spirit. He was no better off. He did not feel his consciousness lifted, did not feel the anger wane even a little.

He let out a long sigh and decided to abandon those thoughts. He stretched out on the turf beneath him. He closed his eyes and would have fallen asleep, now that his adrenaline level was dropping, had not had the strong determination to carry out his mission to the end.

He was reminded of Vanessa and imagined the despair that would seize her upon learning the news.

He had neglected her, Vanessa.

His love of philosophy, history, the Greeks, the Romans, the university, the lectures, the students, the symposia, the talks and conventions, the bullshit and then more bullshit – He had preferred everything to her, his wife, the young girl in Timothy Parker's fruit store, the one who represented the very emblem of beauty, the untouchable touchstone, on a par with the splendid Simonetta Vespucci whom Botticelli immortalized in his most famous paintings, whom he used to depict the face of Primavera, of Venus, with her vaporous femininity, and even the face of the Virgin Mary.

He could never forgive himself for having allowed such intense love to fade away, albeit after so many years, gradually diluting into everyday life to the point of indifference. Without conflict or quarrels. Without arguments or shouting. Simply slipping into indifference, the worst of the shadows that can envelop a heart.

Indifference, disinterest, progressive communication to its eventual death.

All this now seemed implausible.

"How could I?" he asked his *inner self*.

He could not give himself an answer, things had just happened, a succession of events to which he could not even give a sensible time sequence. Everything was so confused, to the point of seeming unreal, as if none of the memories that now crowded his mind had ever really happened. Memory confusing its details with fantasy, confusing reality and imagination.

Vanessa now appeared as a lifeline.

If only he had had her with him for the last seventy-two hours. Nothing terrible could ever have happened if only she had been there.

At that point, suddenly, a spontaneous reaction crept into his thoughts. He decided to stop feeling sorry for himself.

He slowly stood up.

The sun was coming over the horizon, the mission was accomplished and the last decisive step was missing: his handover to the authorities.

He slowly walked toward the 12th Precinct holding the bloody axe in his right hand, now unconsciously, almost as if it had become part of his body.

CHAPTER 32

"Neither to think nor to wish can one,
because the contradiction prevents it."

Dante Alighieri

"Hey, guys. The DNA matches and the toxicology test came in."

Frank O'Brian entered the meeting room where Mark Alessi and Silvio Brugger were, for the umpteenth time, looking at pictures, documents and evidence.

"The data is in the system."

He lifted his clipboard to point to the screens. "Even so… I printed them out. There is something you have to see, and you have to see it *now!*"

Only then did Mark look away from the monitors and turn to Frank. He immediately noticed that the medical examiner's face held an unusual pallor.

He looked tired, but it was not physical exhaustion. It was a moral, deep fatigue, something that had permeated him, had visibly pierced all the way into his spirit like the thin point of a spear.

He read on his face and in his eyes a kind of resignation mixed with darkness and light; he saw the angel and the demon fighting for space on the same tired face.

Frank O'Brian had taken many blows. Every victim that was placed on his ice cold tables aroused in him some anguish.

Over the years, however, he had become accustomed to it in spite of himself; the bar had gradually lowered and he had learned, bit by bit, to regard bodies almost as inanimate mannequins.

The human mind can devise all but perfect self-defense systems; the spirit avoids getting too involved lest it capitulate, lest it be drowned by the whirlwind of strong emotions.

"They should get a psychopath to do this fucking job."

Frank had had this thought on many other occasions, and was entirely serious about it. Of course, because psychopaths are not only serial killers, perpetrators of violence or molesters. A psychopath is primarily a person who has a below-average emotional reception, or even, in the worst cases, no emotional resonance at all. Complete apathy.

"Some companies purposely hire psychopaths," the coroner had realized on more than one occasion, "especially when they feel they need unscrupulous managers."

Sometimes that was what he thought of himself. A man who can accustom himself to death becomes a man without adequate emotional responses. Frank O'Brian, he sometimes believed, had probably become a psychopath himself.

And this was something he could not bear, not if the subject of that progressive numbing of emotions was him.

He had thought many times that it was now too late. The sedation of feelings had already taken place, as slow as it was inevitable, in more than twenty years of working in pathological anatomy. But, all of a sudden, he had an awakening. An awakening of the soul, of feeling, of perception. It had all happened in the worst possible way. Frank O'Brian had rediscovered himself, still alive, still aware of his own emotional perception all because of a helpless body. Or rather two helpless bodies, two child victims, abused and battered.

The ice had shattered, his heart had managed to bleed again, as his eyes moistened and tears began falling at a sight that he had never wished to experience.

All of a sudden he had become *human* again.

"The toxicology exams showed nothing unusual in the girls' bodies. They were not drugged," O'Brian anticipated the reading of the report.

Silvio grabbed the thin folder and handed it to Mark without opening it. He preferred to pull data out of the computer and watch it load on the screens. He wanted the sight of it to be like a slap in the face, from which to draw out the positive anger and determination to continue hounding that damn monster. "On the contrary, the boys seem to have spent the night together. Large amounts of cocaine and alcohol in all three bodies," O'Brian paused, deciding not to go any further.

"A high night, apparently," Silvio interjected sarcastically.

"So Powell might have seen them somewhere, at a party, at a bar and then followed each of them and hunted them down one by one. If we figure out where they spent Friday night, we might find the solution there. Or at least the motive."

Silvio seemed to shoot straight, confident.

He had already tried to figure out how and especially where the murdered boys had spent the evening, and why they were chosen by John Reginald Powell. Now it was evident that the three knew each other and were part of the same group.

On Friday and Saturday evenings, however, almost every venue, restaurant, and bar in New York City has a full house. Going around with photos in hand and asking if anyone had seen them would have been too time-consuming and probably useless.

"There is no need, Silvio." The medical examiner interrupted his thoughts. "Unfortunately, if you look at the DNA test it all becomes pretty damn clear." The papers were in Mark Alessi's hands. The detective opened the folder and pulled out some slides, the ones showing the genetic code compatibility. At that very moment Captain Bishop entered the meeting room.

He looked first at Silvio Brugger and then at Mark Alessi. With his outstretched index finger he pointed to a woman of color in her fifties, with curly black hair and a fearful face.

"See that lady?" he addressed both of them. Despite the fact that the woman was standing about ten meters away, all present company could distinctly see that she was shaking. She was in a state of obvious apprehension and anguish; a nameless fear.

She had heard on TV about the discovery of two little girls' bodies, and her sixth sense as a mother was bringing her to a horrible realisation. An anxious need to know, mixed with deep terror that it might be true. She was wearing a pair of light-colored jeans and a sporty windbreaker. They had seated her in a chair on the side of Detective Brugger's desk.

As soon as she was seated, she gripped her knees with both hands and leaned forward. She was fidgeting, anxious to talk to someone. She had repeated to all the officers that she needed to report an ugly event. An event that she could not comprehend, that was bringing her horror, desolation, confusion and disbelief.

"That lady says she has to report her daughter missing," Captain Bishop paused. Then he continued. "It is likely that we are about to find out the name of the second child."

Silvio looked around with intense discomfort rising in his heart. A sense of duty was telling him that he had to go, but he didn't want to. The same ill-feeling that had seized him when he had been forced to talk to Mr. and Mrs. Bennet at the morgue. Reluctantly, he followed the order of his direct superior and went to collect the lady's complaint. As soon as he had taken his seat, he asked the woman for her personal details and those of the missing child.

The woman spoke her name and her daughter's name in sequence. Silvio was horrified, shocked. His blood ran cold, his fingers froze on the keyboard. His hands, paralyzed, were unable to type the name of the missing child. Detective Brugger suddenly felt blood pulsing in his neck, and rivulets of cold sweat ran down his spine. Just then his colleague, Mark Alessi, was opening the folder with the DNA reports. He stood petrified. He too was shocked, paralyzed at the sudden emergence of the solution to the case.

The truth had arrived like a *tsumani* to upset everyone and everything. It was thrown in the faces of both detectives simultaneously as if there had been a supernatural order directing the succession of events from above.

Four different DNAs had been identified on Alicia Bennet's body. Three of the four organic residues had also been found on the body of *Child 2.*

They matched perfectly. They were perfectly compatible with each other. Identical. But *Child 2* now had a name. Mark had guessed her name from the report. The DNA found on *Child 2's* body was strongly compatible with that of John Reginald Powell but was not his own. NO!

Detective Alessi understood in an instant, and his mind detached. His hands lost their grip and their strength. Papers slid to the floor and fell delicately to the floor. The detective did not care. He looked up at Silvio. Detective Brugger was also staring at his colleague through the glass of the meeting room. The image filtered through the glass made Mark Alessi look like an ethereal, almost transparent figure.

Silvio thought for a second that it was a bad dream. It was a nightmare, it could not be reality. In dreams madness emerges, that madness, as defined by the Greeks, in which you can be everything and the opposite of everything, where there is no principle of noncontradiction and no principle of causality either. In dreams events have no logic, no place. There is no such thing as reason. In dreams there is madness because in dreams you are both spectator and protagonist, you see yourself performing actions, talking, walking, but it is always you watching. Looking at yourself. In dreams, there is no such thing as space-time; the dream can begin two thousand years ago in ancient Rome and end in a glittering New York City of the present day.

But it was not a dream; it was not a dream at all.

The two detectives, burdened by an improper, incomprehensible and persistent pain, stared at each other. Mark continued to hold the folder open but his grip became weak. The ability to hold on faded, he became numb. Papers continued falling slowly from his hand, but it no longer mattered.

Those reports had suddenly become useless. They could lie on the ground; they had already spit out their unfortunate truth. There was no need to pick them up and for a few moments, no one even noticed that they had fallen.

Mark Alessi and Silvio Brugger were motionless for several interminable seconds. Maybe minutes. Of all the resolutions of the case, this one would not have been easy. They breathed deeply, eyes fixed on each other.

Captain Bishop watched the scene without understanding. It was clear that something dramatic was happening, that the detectives were communicating with each other silently, through looks alone. He bent down, picked up the papers Mark Alessi had dropped, and read their contents. On the body of *Child 2*, there were four different DNA codes.

One of them was compatible with John Reginald Powell's but it was not John Reginald Powell's. It was her very own DNA.

CHAPTER 33

*Don't wait for the day you stop suffering because when it comes,
you will know you are dead.*

Tennessee Williams

"Holy Mother of God, Reginald, it is all clear to me now. Now I understand. Everything makes fucking sense now."

John Reginald turned his head slightly over his shoulder and met Mark Alessi's eyes.

"Life is a tremendously ineffable companion, you know Detective?" Powell uttered this sentence brokenly, with the quivering lips of someone about to start weeping again. He stared at Mark softly, imploringly, and his now tired, ravaged and swollen eyes became shiny and wet. Tears soon began running down Powell's face as they had a thousand times in the past few hours. The detective felt that he was now aware, just as his colleagues were, standing silently behind that mirrored glass that invariably furnishes every interrogation room.

"I'll tell you something, Detective," he continued in a broken voice.

"An ancient Roman writer, Publius Ovidius Naso, tells us a famous tale about a boy, Leander, who in order to reach his beloved Ero, swims across the strait of the Hellespont every night. The strait is almost always rough with raging waves and violent currents. He is not discouraged however. With courage and stubbornness he tackles it every night. He calls himself a swimmer on the way out and a castaway on the way back. Shipwrecked because the only real preoccupation, the only torment that darkens his soul, is represented by the time he will be forced to spend away from her on his return."

He lowered his face and wiped his nose and tears, which by now had come copiously to wet his lips and shirt. Mark Alessi let him speak. An intense feeling of compassion began to possess him, and the more he listened to Powell the more that impulse became a thunderous, unbearable tumult that unsettled the aseptic and refractory soul of the police officer, of the FBI detective.

"A father," Powell resumed, "a father would be able to swim across the Hellespont even if it were made of fire, for the love of his daughter."

He burst into tears sobbing loudly for the umpteenth time. He lowered his neck trying to conceal his despair. Dignity did not allow him to show himself fully. His shoulders shook with the sobs of Powell's tormented weeping.

"Shit, Powell. Jamilia… Jamilia was your daughter…," Mark said in a gentle tone, little more than a whisper. Powell had always known that inevitably the painting would be finished; and at that very moment he realized that it was now complete. It had been painted with the most tragic and horrific hues.

"My daughter was only twelve years old, SHE WAS A CHILD, FOR GOD'S SAKE!"

After uttering that excruciating cry, John Reginald Powell's desperate sobs exploded, he began to stutter and heave, and for several minutes all he could do was clutch his head in his hands, his elbows resting on his knees, conspicuously shaking his head in dismay, disbelief, and incomprehension. He would have liked to wake up from that nightmare, to find that it was all just a terrifying dream, but he could not. The sad, stark reality came back to rub that heinous tragedy in his face in every sacred moment. Mark Alessi was frozen. He silently indulged that pain, watching those powerful shoulders jerk, his hands clench his hair, and tears soak his pants.

He was not a serial killer. That man sitting across from him, tormented by unbearable pain, robbed of his own life, ripped from love in a single instant, a man incapable of hate yet filled with it by a terrifying and sudden emptiness.

John Reginald Powell.

Detective Alessi kept staring. He kept seeing the pain of the one he had believed to be a monster approaching. He picked it up, held on to it. The desperate man's pain became his own as well. He could not even begin to imagine what it would feel like to be a man whose child daughter had been murdered, a father whose most beautiful flower, brightest diamond, most unquenchable love had been snatched away. No, he could not imagine it, but he felt his heart tighten all the same, sinking, suffocating. His breath was becoming short, he was struggling to breathe. He turned to the mirror, desperately searching for the support of his colleagues beyond the glass. He could not see them. The mirror proved impenetrable, and he instead discovered from the reflected image that his face was also streaked with tears.

He was crying too. He wiped his face with his palms and lowered his gaze shyly, so as not to be seen crying by his colleagues beyond the glass. They saw him, and neither had the courage to blame him. On the contrary, they were moved.

At the same instant, the movie of his life was unfolding in John Reginald Powell's mind. The last twelve years, the life he had lived with a wonderful daughter, a child who, from the day she was born, had given him her sunny smile, her big, black eyes, of infinite gentleness, goodness and fragility. So much fragility.

"It's easier to die than to see a daughter die," Powell whispered again amid his weeping. Reginald had sunk in the deepest despair and was no longer able to show any rage or malice. The explosion of truth had been a liberation. Liberation from anger and fury. The pain remained. It was the ultimate surrender.

The old lion lying at the foot of the tree and awaiting his fate.

Tears streamed down his face, the movie of his life ran through his mind, the minutes ticked by. Time seemed to have surrendered to pain.

Detective Alessi returned to the man shrouded in darkness. The sunny and happy Louisiana child had become a prisoner in a pit of darkness.

As Alessi continued to stare at him, Powell lifted his head and again showed his tear-soaked face slowly, soaked with pain, his eyes swollen, his brow furrowed.

"You know Detective, a father's love for his daughter is immense even when she is only a baby. And it does not lessen when the child grows up and becomes a young woman. It increases with age, with height; you watch her as her features change, her voice changes, as she grows day by day. But you… you notice that she grows not only in height, not because you notice the changes in her appearance, you don't even notice her voice changing. No, by God. You realize that she is growing because when you hug her, you feel more love, you feel your heart fill with more and more love; the more you watch her grow, the more you feel love grow within you."

The room began to spin. Mark Alessi felt close to breaking down. He stared at Powell, motionless, in a blur. He felt as though he had been struck to the soul. He sensed that he was on the verge of collapse and held on only with great effort.

The walls began to bend, to sway, his mind was invaded by a fog that made him feel like he was in a dream. Or rather a nightmare. The entire interrogation room was swirling around its epicenter: the killer.

This was the scene that now stood before the police officer, the man.

"Her life was still full of dreams... what God could want an end like that for one of his daughters?" Powell continued trying to find a plausible explanation, something that could at least appease that terrible pain; overwhelmed by the most tragic and unbearable malaise that the human soul can suffer. "Now she will forever remain a child. She will be in my memories, because in memories you don't grow up, you don't become an adult, your face does not change or grow older. She will always be my little girl."

It was the same thought he had when he had lost his mother in Baton Rouge. He had left Louisiana as a quiet child and faced life; that same life that was now turning its back on him.

"And then – then I betrayed my promise, Detective. My wife and I are separated. Jamilia stayed over a few days ago, but at night she woke up after a bad dream. I went into her room and hushed her. "Your father is here," I told her. "Your daddy will always be by your side, you have nothing to fear.'"

On the other side of the mirror Silvio Brugger and Simon Bishop stood frozen. They had not moved a single finger in the past fifteen minutes. No one could have sensed even their breathing. They seemed to be in apnea, paralyzed.

"Victim comes from the Latin *victima*, 'sacrifice,'" Captain Bishop whispered as he closed his eyes. "Who is the victim in all this? And who is the executioner?" He turned imperceptibly toward Silvio.

"Sometimes I think revenge is, in a way, a necessary feeling, you know Captain?" replied Brugger. "A relief valve for society, some distinguished man said... but, honestly, now I can't even remember who it was."

Mark, meanwhile, had started walking slowly and nervously around the table in the room where John Reginald Powell had brought up the greatest sorrow among great sorrows, the most desperate cry among desperate cries.

"Friday morning she was supposed to go to school. She went down to the street and waited for the school bus on the sidewalk. She always did that. I was at the window waving to her. But then that car stopped. Three boys got out and took her."

Reginald's gaze was fixed in the void. It seemed as if an automaton in his tired body was speaking.

"They were shouting, they were definitely drunk, high. I rushed down the stairs but when I got there the car was already leaving." He drew a deep breath. At that moment, a smile of derisive self-pity was plastered on his face. "But I got the license plate, you know detective? I got it, I got it...."

Time remained suspended, the air still for a few interminable seconds. "That's exactly why, Powell. That's why you remain a fucking serial killer, for God's sake!", Mark Alessi suddenly broke that unreal silence. "And you will end up in front of a federal judge."

He took the handcuff keys from his pocket and unfastened John Reginald's wrists.

"You killed three men, and that cannot be done in New York. In the United States of America you can't do that, even if you kill three bastard spoiled boys who raped and killed your daughter," Detective Alessi kept raising his voice.

He was venting all the frustration of the moment, the sense of oppression, he needed to lighten his soul, throw off that heavy weight that took his breath away.

"You're going to rot in a fucking federal prison. That's where we throw shitty murderers like you. You can't do justice for yourself, not here in New York."

Detective Mark Alessi seemed to be reborn as a phoenix from the ashes, but he was overflowing with anger and resentment. He had solved five murders in one, but the news did not cheer him at all. The lives cut short remained.

Massacre.

He grabbed Powell by the arm. He was aware that that tall, massive set of muscles could have thrown him off in a second, perhaps beaten him and rebelled. But Reginald did not. Mark knew he would not because John Reginald Powell had in his eyes now a dull light, soulless and empty. On his face were the signs of unconditional defeat to an existence that could never again be his. Mark opened the door suddenly and threw Powell into the hallway with a vigorous push from behind. Reginald was on the verge of falling, despite his size. Powell turned around, stunned, with a look full of questioning and unable to realize what Alessi was doing; he did not understand.

"I'll throw you in a cell, you old son of a bitch!"

Now the abuse, the insults, the shoving seemed to go over the top. Mark was losing his temper, everything he had held inside seemed about to explode. Exhaustion, frustration, resentment.

Silvio Brugger and Captain Bishop saw the two disappear around the corner of the corridor. They listened to Mark's expletives for a few seconds, turning to each other with a questioning expression.

"What's going on with him?" the Captain asked Silvio, Mark Alessi's lifelong friend. "Mark is an Italian, Captain, a sanguine. He occasionally loses his temper. At least that's what I think."

At exactly the same time, John Reginald Powell and Mark Alessi entered the corridor where the three cells were located. Mark held Powell by the arm and pushed him forward. He had not put the handcuffs back on the suspect; great recklessness.

They arrived at cell number one; they carried on. Two; they carried on.

Mark gave John Reginald a harder shove than the others, forcing him past cell number 3 and into a side corridor.

At the bottom was a small, gray, metal door with a green panic bar handle.

Mark Alessi quickened his pace and positioned himself in front. Reaching the door first, he opened it. "Well, it's not locked."

Night had just invaded the sky with its stars. That city of chiaroscuro now seemed as magnificent as when Powell arrived there with his father from Louisiana; it was so sparkling and promising. The hallway was suddenly invaded by a blast of new, clean, fresh air that quickly replaced the foul air in the district's rooms. Powell drew a deep breath and closed his eyes. He did not understand the meaning of the detective's gesture and remained motionless, enjoying the cool rush in his lungs and on his damp skin.

"Hey, champ." Mark unexpectedly showed a sort of inexplicable affection toward the man that he could never have imagined the day before. He placed both hands on his biceps. He squeezed to convey a feeling of closeness. Almost friendship.

"Just punch me and run away, I'll take care of the rest."

Reginald was bewildered, almost stunned. "I can't Detective. I thank you but I can't. I wouldn't know where to go, I wouldn't know what to do. My soul is completely torn by grief, an unbearable burden. What kind of life would I live? And then what should I do? Run away forever? Watch my back every moment with the fear of being caught? And for what?"

"I understand that Reginald. I understand that, and I stand by you. But you still have someone to take care of. You definitely have to take care of a great man, a brave one, one with a kind soul, filled with love and passion. You have to take care of yourself, Reginald."

Powell burst into yet another heartbreaking cry. "What do you want me to do, Detective? That I become a man in constant search of a reason to justify his own existence?"

This time it was the black giant who caught Mark Alessi from behind with both big hands. Imploring, Powell came within inches of the detective's face. Mark scrutinized its every wrinkle, the signs of the passage of time, the marks of a busy and full life.

"Let's go back in, please. Don't compromise your position as well, Detective," John Reginald urged him.

"Compromise my position, you say? I am already compromised, Reginald. My heart and soul are already terribly compromised, because both are on your side. I am betraying the basic principles of justice. My heart is compromised because it tells me that you did the right thing, that you got three sons of bitches out of the way who maybe, thanks to family money, would have even gotten away with it in a federal court. I am compromised. I am compromised because my convictions have rotted. Justice is, and must remain, a clean affair. That's what my brain tells me. But the heart, well... my heart is now compromised because it is with you, Powell, it is on your side without a shadow of a doubt."

He stared into his eyes with the fire of a red sunset and, at the same time, with the tender benevolence of a father.

John Reginald Powell understood the sincere impetus, the deep emotion, and the candid and shameless frankness of the words with which Mark Alessi had bared his soul.

"You have already paid, Powell. You paid in advance and you paid a hefty bill. You would find no ransom, no remedy in a federal prison. No punishment could ever be inflicted on you, more punitive and painful than the one you already carry in your heart." Powell believed him. He believed the sincerity of those words. He felt a faint, thin thread of hope rise in his heart.

It was at first almost imperceptible; then suddenly it erupted like lava, exploding with the same violence with which the anger of the previous days had exploded.

"Now go, run. Punch me and run as fast as you can, fly away like the wind, evaporate, disappear."

He did not make it in time.

Powell turned around and saw that Detective Silvio Brugger and Captain Simon Bishop were standing still, halfway down the hall. The captain had not yet realized what he was seeing, and in doubt, he shifted his jacket and slowly brought a hand to the gun in the holster.

Silvio was also on the verge of grabbing the gun, confused by the scene he did not yet grasp. Seconds passed. Then Bishop guessed; he placed his left hand on Silvio Brugger's arm with the clear purpose of blocking his colleague.

Reginald watched them for several interminable moments without being able to realize exactly what to do. For a moment he stood motionless. He raised his arms in surrender. With bated breath.

With one foot on the door and the other out on the street, ready to savor freedom again and yet stuck there, planted, compressed, squeezed between a new instinct for survival and a dramatic and painful new outlook on life. Adding to this was the fear that Captain or Detective Brugger might give free rein to their guns.

Mark, too, turned and met his colleagues' incredulous expressions. He directed them with a subtle gaze, eyelids, tired and pleading.

The captain still kept one hand on the gun and the other on Brugger's right arm. Their eyes met. Subtle, silent, yet loaded with meaning. Neither the Captain nor Silvio moved a single finger. The message was clear, unequivocal.

Detective Alessi understood this on the fly and went back to Powell, grabbed his face in his hands, rested their foreheads together. His eyes moistened and let two small tears flow. Then, in a moved voice he said to him, "Go away now, Reginald. And don't let me see you again."

He relinquished his grip, shifted slightly to his left, and pushed John Reginald Powell out the door with the last of many forceful shoves, the only one really appreciated by both Powell and Detective Mark Alessi. He disappeared, John Reginald Powell.

Just as unexpectedly and incredibly he had entered the department, he was now leaving it. The glittering, shining New York decided that for one evening it would remain dark and silent, that it would turn off its myriad lights and muffle its extravagant sounds to swallow, in silence, the darkness and pain of one of its countless adopted children.

Mark slowly lowered himself and sat down on the step below the doorway. Silvio joined him, slipped a cigarette out of his pocket, lit it with an indolent movement, and sat down next to him.

They remained with their gaze fixed on emptiness, each immersed in their own thoughts.

Then Silvio threw the cigarette to the ground and crushed it with a quick movement of his foot from right to left and back. He lifted his arm and passed it over his friend's head. He accompanied the gesture by turning toward him. He embraced him. Mark turned, returned the hug and let a couple of shy tears furrow his face before letting them drop on Silvio Brugger's shirt.

The mighty silhouette of John Reginald Powell had disappeared into the darkness. But he would not disappear forever. He would leave an indelible mark of his own passing.

On the hearts and souls of detectives Mark Alessi and Silvio Brugger.